THE
HALF-
MOTHER

EMMA TENNANT

THE HALF-MOTHER

Little, Brown and Company
Boston   Toronto

For Tim

PART ONE

1

Sun came through today. The kitchen filled up first, with pale orange stripes on red walls and Moura's blue-and-green porcelain cups going suddenly the colour of the sea outside. Lily's hair shines out as frizzy as a lamb as she walks from the dishwasher (broken again) to the chipped wooden edge of the sink. Ten days of low mist, since the discovery in the leaves, the rush of steps and the long cars, and the standing under a sky spotted like a plastic umbrella. Lily turns to face me, in a blaze of light.

'The pot, Minnie. Where's the pot?'

I am such a fool. I laid my hand on the top of the kitchen cabinet, where 'the boys'' latest presents to Moura stand in the usual jumble of string and old envelopes: a wooden fetish – from one of the Caribbean Islands, no doubt, where Philip goes to show up the latest corrupt regime and, quite useless, this, a riding crop (expensive) with the card saying '*love Gareth and Fran*' still half attached to the handle. Moura would never take it out with her. She gave up hunting years ago anyway – had they forgotten? – and likes to ride bareback, alone, on the hills up away from the sea. I looked down at my hand, slatted white by the sun.

'I don't know what you mean, Lily.'

'It must've been yesterday, when I wasn't in. Oh, for God's sake, Minnie, what is Mrs Pierce going to say?'

She found the broken pot in the bin, then. But I don't care. 'I only put my hand down here,' I said. That Chinese porcelain pot – it matches the cups – it has a pretty bamboo handle – but then I'm such a fool.

'She won't think it was you, Lily.' My tone doesn't console. 'You know it's the kind of thing that always happens to me.'

'Yes it is, but you tell her all the same.' Lily moved out of the light and I saw how the last ten days have aged her. Her stoop at the sink is an old woman's. Her cheeks are sunk in. Or maybe it's that everything looks different in these days of shock. Even the clock face on the wall offers a new expression. And the calendar – Lily's head part-obscures it now, as she scrubs at the sink – the calendar with its silly, coloured view of the Galway coast, seems to come from another world.

'Where is Mrs Pierce then?' I went to the window, pretended to look out at the terraced cliff garden and the sea beyond, pale today as milk poured in a bottle. You can just make out the hills opposite, across the estuary. When the bottle empties and the sea rushes out, a wide, sandy beach comes up in front of the caravans.

I knew where Moura was, of course. Beards of dead palm had blown on to the grass by the window, which is so low you can step out of it on to a wedge of ground over the cliff. She was clearing – you could hear the thwack of the axe.

'She's in the wild garden,' Lily said. 'Go on, then, Minnie, get out of my kitchen.'

And her eyes filled with tears, she pulled a shard of blue-and-green porcelain from her apron pocket (so she'd been hiding it there all along) 'Mr Hugo liked his tea out of this,' she said.

If I spent my life trying, I could never do justice to the beauties of Cliff Hold – and of Dunane generally. Perhaps it's because I came here as a child that the pattern of lanes, stiff with fuchsia in summer and open to the sky in winter, seems unrepeatable, perfect; the slope of the house on the high rock above the sea; the village you reach by following the purple lanes and going down so your legs ache to the harbour wall, have the exactness of perspective of a dream.

From the village of Dunane one can only look up with awe at Cliff Hold. Not that it's so big – it's more the effrontery of building so far out on the rock, and making a staircase of the garden. And the other thing about the house: it's as far along the cliff as you can go. From Moura's bedroom window, which juts out in a little box like a prie-dieu and holds her desk and her favourite paintings, you can see grey waves – and no hills on the other side of the bay – they've been left far behind in the race for the open sea. The nearest neighbour is America. Sea birds hover outside Moura's window and she'll look up quickly from her desk. Sometimes I think she sees her sons in them, coming back across the Atlantic, beating against the glass to be let in. But it's that kind of thinking that leads me into trouble – and now Moura, standing a little breathless from her clearing of untidy sub-tropical trees, resting on the axe, says:

'You are an idiot, Minnie. Don't mention it.'

'But . . . I'd like to replace it. I mean . . .' Blundering again – a Chinese porcelain teapot owned by Moura is obviously irreplaceable.

Moura pushed back her hair, still the pale yellow of the portrait in her room at Cliff Hold, and opened her hands wide. 'Look how much I've done this afternoon.'

Moura is as hard to describe as the house and the village and the cliff. She seems tall from far away and then is surprisingly small when you're near – not very much smaller than I am, I mean to say, but much smaller than Fran, her daughter-in-law, Gareth's wife. Her face is quite lined but very beautiful and determined-looking. Her hair, as I said, is pale yellow like the silk in the Oriental hangings on her bedroom wall. I couldn't say about her eyes. They are smaller, too, than you think – they might be grey.

'Hugo liked tea out of that pot.'

Moura made no effort to reply to my latest clumsiness. The axe swung, a self-seeded, unwanted sapling went down on to the grass. She stopped and began to pull off the slender branches. I stood staring – at the white cicatrice on the mottled bark, the handful of earth still clinging to the roots of the tree. Over Moura's back the drop to the sea was pure vertigo. The beach, miles down, was exposed: it was low tide. There were no children on the strand, though. September: holidays over; the caravans were deserted, empty boxes of aluminium.

Why didn't I turn and walk back to the house? I had only to collect my bag and go down the steep lane to the bus stop outside Ryan's pub. Lily wouldn't be leaving for hours yet – after doing the kitchen she had the passage to mop down (the mosaic passage, laid in smooth, pale-blue and white pebbles by Moura – an expression of her eccentric good taste, her not caring what others might think). And then there was Gareth, lying ill in the last bedroom off the passage where it turns to the left. Lily would give him tea. She would be in there a long time, plumping his pillows and talking to him as she had when he was a child – when Lily's soft voice was so much more comforting than Moura's strident English. I could walk down, sit in Ryan's until the bus came.

I didn't. My sense of mis-timing is famous. Or is time away from Cliff Hold always mis-time? Is Cliff Hold – and the village down there by the beach, the intricate pattern of white houses, the Catholic church ('that's the *Catholic* church,' Moura says to visitors when she takes them on a tour), the only place I've ever felt at home? Strange, when until ten days ago I hadn't been here for ten years. 'I think I'll go for a walk,' I say instead.

Moura straightens. She clutches the torn-off branches and tenses her arms. As the wood shoots down on to the ledge where Moura accumulates her rubbish, burning it at night so that ships coming in see a bright rag of fire, a dangerous will o' the wisp to lure them on to the most vicious rocks on the coast, Moura turns to me with a smile. You could almost swear she was happy – but she can't be, of course, only ten days after Hugo's death.

'I'll come with you.'

My heart sinks, but then she was bound to say that. Now she puts her hand up over her eyes and looks out to sea. 'I think we could get a razor clam or two if we went down to the beach. Come on, Minnie.'

Half-way down the path, Moura stops again. And I almost push her over, stopping suddenly, heavily on her heels.

'Damn!' Moura looks over her shoulder, smiling. 'We forgot the salt. We'll have to go back to the house.'

'The salt?' At that moment, in the jungle undergrowth, in the moistness of a September afternoon, under wide leaves and ferns that blocked out the sun and closed me with Moura in an underwater nowhere,

13

I felt only stunned. The option I'd refused – the walk down the white lane between the bright hedges to the street in Dunane, the litter of cardboard cups by the bus stop – the blunt-nosed bus that would take me to Cork, and so to the airport and home – the sense of a last chance gone, held me close to Moura, under the thick leaves.

'Yes, the salt. You remember, Minnie. You used to do it when you were a child.'

'Oh, yes.'

Moura started to climb again. Some sun came through on to her shoulders: we must be getting near the 'clearing'. Moura goes on talking for she never gets out of breath.

'You make a depression in the sand at low tide. You fill it with salt. And the razor clam thinks the tide is coming in. It's the only way to catch them.'

'Yes, I remember.'

It sounds so heartless, somehow. But do razor clams matter? Aren't I really remembering the times I went on the strand with Philip, when Moura had given him salt to catch a razor clam and he ran laughing to the sea with it and threw it in? Moura must have picked up my thoughts, for she said: 'Philip's coming soon. I'm quite sure of it.'

We've passed the 'clearing' and reached the jagged stone steps up to the house. Bushes of lavender give off a strong scent: as we walk a cloud of small bees rises and then settles again. The house, forbidding to look up at from the village of Dunane, shows long windows you can't see from down there: windows that are open and lead to the drawing-room, Moura's vases of peonies and mignonette and the heavy pine mantelpiece Hugo used to lean against. Further along is the kitchen: no sign of Lily moving about there. She must have gone in to Gareth by now.

14

'Gareth came here after all,' I said.

Moura pulls off a sprig of lavender. She holds it up to the light. The sun doesn't make much difference to the lavender, though – it doesn't sparkle or anything like that – and Moura hastily holds it to her nose. 'Philip will be here soon, Minnie. He sent a cable.' She sniffs long and luxuriously at the lavender as she speaks. 'Oh darling, isn't it all beautiful here?' She waves her arms, the sprig falls to the ground, she smiles in soft complacency at having achieved a defence of her eldest son again. 'Will you pop in and fetch the salt, Minnie? The silver salt-cellar in the dining-room, it pours better . . .'

So here I am, going down to the beach by the lane – it's quicker that way. After the hedges, the neat bunga-lows, the front gardens where men with red faces mow the grass. Then the narrow lane down to the harbour wall . . . the low, white houses painted a bright white over mud, like dung-caked swallows' nests in a row. From a bungalow garden where a woman sits in a deckchair I hear a laugh. And as we go, children squeal out in laughter from the black interiors of the houses in the white row. Now we come to the steps in the wall. We're near the main street of Dunane, the old men going into Ryan's Bar, the women in green raincoats going to Mr Ryan's shop next door. I hear the laughter, as we sink from their sight on to firm, still-wet sand under the wall. I do look a fool, of course, walking just a few steps behind Moura and carrying a Georgian silver salt-cellar with a fancy top like a pagoda. But I could have chosen the other way – walked down the lane alone and carrying my bag, and waited for the bus to take me out of Dunane.

2

I was at my mother's in North Kensington when she told me Hugo was dead.

My mother is a maths tutor – and so, in a feeble way, am I (children under nine, smart new pencil case in hand, the long silence as the mind wanders and the plane trees outside my mother's Crescent flat seem to block all future thought). The overhead light with the dark shade was on, I remember, at an earlier hour than usual. It was one of those still, late August days when the leaves on the trees look as if they've decided to hang on for ever and to turn a dark, spinach green. The shade added to the gloom. I had decided to switch to a little English coaching, to make the fractions and the long division more bearable. These children were supposed to go on to an expensive private school.

My mother walked straight in, paying no attention to the 'Bells . . . ' 'What do bells do?' Bells . . . 'Yes, bells chime, or bells ring . . . bells ring . . . what do they do?' She stood by the lino-covered table, a pile of exercise books swept off by her skirt to the floor. It is rare for my mother to show any excitement on these dismal occasions and I stopped and looked up at her, pen in hand.

'Hugo was found . . . '

'Found?'

For a moment we gaped at each other. An eight-year-old in grey shorts wriggled in his chair.

'Found dead . . . in a wood.' My mother turned and went abruptly to the window. She looked out at the plane trees, and the first stallholders setting up for the Friday market: quilts smelling of cat, brass stilettos, opaline jugs.

'You mean his body was found?'

My mother swung round in exasperation. How I madden her; but I always have. Moura was kind to me when I was a child, kinder than my mother; Moura was my mother really, I suppose.

'Yes. His body. Thank you.'

It was important, though, to make the distinction. With Hugo particularly. For he was all mind – when his mind was tired his large, shambling body simply refused to understand instructions. At mealtimes it would wander into the study next to Gareth's room at the end of the passage at Cliff Hold, instead of into the dining-room, where Moura waited by the plates. When he was alert his body would walk for miles right up on to the long hills by Ardo.

My mother might have been reading my thoughts. Or she knows, anyway, where my thoughts usually are. A long way from the crossroads and the pub opposite our flat where the night brawls are followed by sirens and scuffles – and hundreds of miles from the stalls outside, with their flimsy awnings that don't keep out the rain. My mother used to tease me about my thoughts, until she saw I couldn't bear it any longer. After all, it was she who had taken me to Dunane, left me there for long summers when she went to France and married; and winters when you couldn't see the white sea birds for the mist over the cliff and she'd gone away again, to Mexico this time, with a man who wasn't even the new husband. You wouldn't think it now, looking at my stout mother in

17

the flat with the green lino and the piles of exercise books. You wouldn't think she'd ever known a man.

'He was found in the woods at Ardo,' she said.

I went out of the room without looking back – at the round, fair head of the eight-year-old still seated at the table, or at my mother who had gone back to the window. I went down the stairs, past the Regency peeling wallpaper that was so unlike anything Moura would have allowed near her. It was only when I walked out into the street that I realized I had to make myself ready to go. I couldn't just walk out like this, like you can at Cliff Hold, taking the steps and the path down to the beach at low tide, or starting down to the village and then branching left up a field, past the ruins of the old abbey and the Protestant churchyard where Hugo now lies. It's strange I should have been transported so completely, after ten years. But I was. I stood outside the front door of the converted Edwardian house in North Kensington and I saw the sea, and then the hall at Cliff Hold, Moura's long flower basket and a pile of old boots that Philip and Gareth had worn. I smelt the sea.

A man half fell over my legs, setting up a pavement stall. He emptied velvet bags of tarnished silver spoons and made a rough display. I turned back into the house, but not until I'd rung the bell and my mother had pressed the buzzer to open the door. I'd left my key, my bag, everything.

Moura has taken possession of the salt-cellar. She walks ahead on the sand; the wrinkled sand, the pale gold colour, the washed-out blue of the sea are the materials Moura is made of. In her faded cotton skirt are holes, which show her bare legs, brown from the summer. Her lined, curious face peers down at indentations in the sand, as if a fish, or a miraculous shell

18

might come up to her. Finally she kneels, making two kneecaps of wet sand.

'Here, Minnie. You remember. Make a scoop.'

The cold, wet sand on my legs made me feel sick when I knelt down. I scrabbled with my fingers and grit came up under the nails. I saw Philip so strongly then, standing hands in pockets with his back to Dunane and his head facing America. Anyone could have realized he'd go there – to make his fortune, to take a whole new continent by storm. Of course our engagement had been a children's thing. Hugo, the famous writer, the man of letters, the man with the dispassionate eye, had seen that and advised Philip to go while there was still time. (I hadn't known, then, that Hugo was all these things. I knew he wrote books, of course: journalists came to interview him and Moura sent Lily out on the lawn with drinks.) But it was my mother, when I came back to London (her own last marriage had just broken up and she was sighing in the flat, starting her tutoring in order to pay the bills, sending me out for red, shiny exercise books that were cheaper if you went all the way to the City and bought them in bulk) who said as I stood there crying by the eternal plane trees on another August night ten years ago: 'But Minnie, I knew your engagement wouldn't last long. Hugo is far too ambitious to allow Philip to throw himself away on a girl like you.'

Now Moura pulls impatiently at my hand. I think suddenly: her fingers are claws, she's a crab that moves sideways to get its prey. But I shouldn't think that. I'll always look after Moura. Her scuttling fingers meet mine under the sand.

'There. Your scoop wasn't nearly deep enough. Now take this.' She hands over the salt-cellar. 'Go on. Shake some in.'

'How much?' I felt so stupid again: even making a

hole in the sand I get it wrong. Moura laughed. It's such a pleasant laugh. 'Just enough to fool a razor clam.'

I shake the silver, perforated lid so hard that it flies off and a pile of salt is deposited on the sand: the base quickly turns grey.

'Minnie! Honestly!'

But my clumsiness was more opportune than I knew. Moura's head was low, she was pushing the salt, mixed with sand now, into the base of the silver pot. Perhaps, unconsciously, I was trying to save her, protect her for another few seconds from the sight of the two men walking towards us over the sand. Moura restored the lid of the salt-cellar and delicately sprinkled the scoop as if it was a half-eaten egg. And I think . . . I think against the sound of the steps of the men on the wrinkled face of the sand: this is mad; it's too late to fool a clam, anyway; the tide is coming in.

Those long, shallow minutes when you're waiting for something to happen, or something has happened and you can't know it yet – when you float on the top of time – I see the sea coming in slowly, in thin half-moons of dull water overlapping. I look up at the sky and see clouds forming at last in the pale blue. Cliff Hold seems to rise straight out of rock from here, the elaborate gardens are concealed, on show only to the ocean, to ships coming in from the west.

I think of the churchyard, the burial of Hugo. There's Gareth – he's slight and fair, everyone says he looks exactly like Moura. He doesn't, of course: it's just that he isn't the image of Hugo – as Philip is. There, standing beside him at the edge of the grave, is Lily – Lily wearing an obedient look, as if death, her master, has come and she had always known he would – even to the man whose shoes she cleaned and whose shirts she thumped in a tub because the washing machine was broken again. Where's Fran? It's all very well for Gareth to stand next to the old woman who held him in her arms while Moura went painting along the western shores – but he's married now. Where's Fran?

Moura looks up. Before she sees the shadow of the men – or maybe she senses it – she leans towards me urgently.

'Minnie!'

I don't answer; I seem to be staring out to sea. Clouds have packed in now, and turned an evening grey so that sea and sky are the colour of absence – Fran's absence at the side of the grave – and, most of all, Philip's. How could he not have come?

I don't know if I could ever explain Hugo. I know that he and Moura were friends of my mother before the war – in Moura's photograph albums it looks a glamorous scene. Hugo the Communist, the brilliant needler of the Establishment, already then a praised novelist, 'a man like an eighteenth-century man', a friend of my mother once said – and when I asked him what that meant he said Hugo was like someone born before the birth of self-consciousness, anxiety, doubt. You can see Hugo and my mother and Moura and the man my mother married after she got rid of my father – and writers and painters in the baggy jerseys and short hair of the 1930s – and rich girls in white mink jackets – all sitting at the cocktail bar in the house Moura had rented in London for the summer before the war. The picture was exciting and far away. And when Hugo moved at the outbreak of war to Ireland, and Moura's family evicted two ancient cousins from Cliff Hold and made the house over to the new couple, there was time for writing the novels – and the international reputation grew.

What is it about the novels? They read like simple

adventure stories, but people tell me I'm not subtle enough to see the other levels they're really working on. Like an amused vision of despair . . . a rejection of 'compassion', Hugo's most hated word. My mother described them like that to me when I was fifteen, and had just come back from a long summer at Dunane: her Sunday newspaper tones rang round the bijou house she owned in Belgravia at the time. 'My dear, Hugo may be awarded the *Nobel* Prize! Just adventure stories, I ask you! No, Minnie – it's the *condition humaine* . . . '

I remember I went upstairs and lay on the bed in the chintzy room I was allowed to use when my mother didn't have friends from Mexico or France. I'd had a long summer on the beaches and coves with Philip – fishing for mackerel, hours spent after dark on the rocks – climbing in through a ground-floor window at Cliff Hold because Moura had locked the main door. I wasn't interested in Hugo's novels at all.

All the same, no one lasted long without falling in love with Hugo. The word for him was lovable – you heard it wherever you went (except for Ryan's Bar where the love for Hugo was so great it needed no word: if Hugo was sitting with his glass of Paddy and his eyes trained on the wide, plate glass window and the sea and the gulls – 'always a better vantage point than the one from home' – there was laughter, almost applause: Hugo likes his drink). But it was odd he should have seemed so lovable to the very people he wrote about regularly in his novels: the American bankers and the Anglo-Irish hunting set, the rich and the mindless who served mayonnaise-with-everything in their just-bought or inherited – magnificently refurbished or decrepit – castles and manor houses in the South. Why didn't they hate him, when he so transparently took them as his models for the

Seven Deadly Sins? (*Captain Sloth* he set in South Africa, but the Captain was modelled on a near neighbour, a fervent champion of apartheid; the *Earl of Greed* he sent as a prospector to one of the last remaining beautiful and unspoilt areas of jungle in the world; *Rex Envy*, who killed to get his friend's wife and then fell out of love, was clearly based on the incalculably rich Texan who had bought Castle Carne after Lord Carne's mysterious death, married Lady Carne and then sent her packing.) Why didn't they mind? Why, in fact, did they go on inviting him – and with undimmed pleasure? Hugo was a great enlivener, of course – and Moura was beautiful – and most of these people were bored stiff: he was like the bitters that turned their gin the colour of a good hunting pink. Hugo was lovable. How would he surprise them next?

Hugo made me love him when I realized, thanks to his apparently effortless attentions, that to be a child wasn't necessarily to be boring. I'd grown up in the shadow of my mother's yawns; her friends, multivaried as they were and depending on who she was married to at the time, didn't seem to know how to deal with my presence at all. The literary friends were unable to cope with my ignorance. The jet-set friends saw I was plain and badly dressed. I spent all my time in one bedroom or another, reading the books my mother had brought back from her journeys: travel books that smelt of tobacco, love novels that had a sickening smell of chocolate gone stale. I didn't see myself in any of these books and saw the world, consequently, from a frightening angle: it took Hugo, with his laughter at the ways of the world, his rapid explanations of people's characters and motives – and all this done partly as a joke – for me to see myself at all. (In a favourable light, too, as the recipient of Hugo's jokes about others.)

23

By the time I was old enough to be taken into his confidence – and, of course, to have fallen in love with Philip, who was so like his father in speech and appearance that he seemed sometimes a thinner, lighter copy – by the time I was old enough to stay up late at night and go into his study for a talk after Philip and I came back from fishing or cycling, I would certainly have done anything for Hugo. Not that he ever needed much, except a refill of whiskey or a nip down to Ryan's for more tobacco for his pipe – they'd hand tobacco out the door at any hour, if it was for Hugo Pierce.

So I don't know which of the memories was the strongest, of all those that pulled me out to Dunane again after ten years: Hugo's, who I couldn't believe I would never see again; or Moura's, who I felt must urgently need me. Her voice was faint when I rang from my mother's flat, since having to be let in after my first panicky flight into the street.

'Who? Oh . . . good heavens . . . Minnie.'

My mother stood by the lino-covered table, making a disapproving face. The door bell rang; the mother of the eight-year-old had come to take him home.

'I'm so sorry about Hugo.' I couldn't think of anything else to say.

'What . . . what . . . are you coming, Minnie?'

So she did need me. I had enough money – just – to take a plane to Cork. My eyes slanted to the table, to the boy in grey shorts picking up his books.

'In a wood . . . yes, in the wood. You know it, Minnie, the woods at Ardo.'

The sound of the place made me feel happy then. Yet what I see most clearly of that moment is the boy's exercise books, the ruled lines and the words that no longer meant anything to me.

I packed and flew to Cork. Moura was waiting at the

airport. That was ten days ago. Now the Guards who've been crossing the sand are stooping, speaking politely to Moura who is still on her knees by the incoming tide. Would Mrs Pierce like to come up to Cliff Hold just for a little minute? Would I like to come too?

Moura looks up at me, not at them.

'Minnie!'

This time I turn to her, nod as if we've been expecting the Guards all along.

'Minnie, where's Fran?' Moura says. 'I haven't seen her; she should be back by now.' She gazed up expectantly at the men. 'Do tell me – have *you* seen Fran? Mrs Gareth Pierce?'

The steps in the wall. The Guards' black boots are wet, shirred with sand. The sea has come in under the wall where it goes into rocks under Cliff Hold. The sea has thrown a scarf of black and green seaweed on to the wall. I might run along the wall and throw myself into the sea. But the water is still shallow there, in a cauldron with lumps of bony rock and floating weed. I would thrash about, the top half of me humiliatingly exposed, like the lobsters Moura throws in the pot to boil.

This way, you don't have to go past the white mud houses or the bungalows: you just go up and up, in steep steps to the lane by Cliff Hold. The climb makes the legs ache – Hugo used to say he was always telling Ryan to move his pub up the hill. The lungs begin to heave (not Moura's, of course: she looks down at me with composure as we climb). The village of Dunane pops up below us – there's the church, there are the houses in their gardens – but it's the Catholic church that lies below us, next to Ryan's pub. I see Mrs Ryan in her new camel-hair coat, crossing from the store and going into the church. Suddenly I wonder . . . why is the church door open like that? Would they . . . carry anyone in there? No. Of course not. And I think, it's so long since I've been in Ireland it could be the South of Italy or Spain. Surely – if someone – was hurt – or – had been shot – wounded . . .

'Minnie, I keep wondering where Fran can be.'

Surely – the steps beat the breath from me as I climb – surely – they'd be taken to hospital – like – they do at home.

3

I first met Fran when we were both at film school. The narrow, wooden steps in the old warehouse in Covent Garden literally threw us together one day – Fran was going up, with a great pack of equipment on her back, and I was running down. In the classic movie style, Fran's pack went flying: I helped pick it up and in ten minutes we were friends. That was eleven years ago. Fran knew only a few people in London, my mother was at that time well off and married to her Mexican count – or in the last throes of her marriage without knowing it – and I asked this tall, smiling American girl to come home and have a meal. For a while, everything went like a Cary Grant movie after that. Fran had luck, or charm, or whatever it is you can never work for. She calmed people and galvanized them into action at the same time. Her long, black hair made a perfect V in the middle of her smooth, white forehead. She was perfect. When she was older, and I heard of the bravery of her film news expeditions to places ravaged with war and disease – Beirut, Gambia, Afghanistan – I could imagine the crippled and the ill obeying Fran's camera instructions. You just had to do what she said.

I didn't stay long at the film school and nor did Fran. My reasons were that my mother became all at once penniless and we had to start on our uneven, hustling life (by hustling I mean that my mother used to send me round to the rich people she had known long ago and get me to ask for money: this only stopped after I burst out crying one day when the rich woman in question, in her Eaton Square flat, gave me a pound note and opened the door to show me out. Which finally distressed my mother). Fran's reasons for leaving the school were that she was offered, from the States, the job of editing news film as it came through London, to make up documentary films for TV. She would eventually be able to make films of her own, if she made a success of it. From a student operating worn-out machinery in the film school, making 'shorts' that won acclaim but were always considered rather 'heavy' by the other students, she was propelled into the grown-up world. I went to see her in her editing room, where she was poring over footage from countries in the hold of starvation, illness, death. I wondered why she didn't tie back her long hair as it kept getting in the controls of the machine. As she stopped and speeded the images, the veil of soft black hair came down over frozen mountains, legless stumps of mountain men fighting for their high villages, rubble of burning hospitals and children whose eyes would never recover from what they had seen. Fran seemed screened off now from our ordinary world, by her hair that shut her in with these satellite images of suffering and pain.

27

Fran was rich. In our early days as friends I didn't know this: the anonymity of jeans, sweatshirts, boots and leather bag with tassels and beads protected her from envy, from being set apart. When we went out together she had as little money as I – and I assumed, like everyone else, that her fees at the film school were paid by some overseas grant. In those days, anyway, the last winds of pretended freedom, liberty and easily held radical beliefs were still blowing (though they wouldn't blow for much longer) and the subject of money was never raised. Fran was just a part of the scene; many of the men we knew had hair as long and silky as she and walked with the same fastidious, narrow-waisted gait. If some of us saw a special quality in Fran, we put it down to her being an American woman at the outset of the great feminist revolution. It was sometimes said that Fran was more open, had fewer inhibitions, a stronger sense of her identity and future than her English counterparts: that was true, certainly, but it wasn't resented. The women among us felt inspired by Fran's easy mastery of any situation that came up. The men, wary of calm and competence in an intelligent woman at a time when intelligent women were questioning themselves and their expectations as never before, admired Fran and stood to one side. It was as if they knew a New Man was needed to partner this New Woman (for that is what Fran appeared to be – a member of a new species of a distant continent, a species that lacked masochism, dependence, vulnerability – woman's traditional ills). This New Man had not yet evolved. Such was the nonsense we all talked and thought in those days long ago – but, as is often the case with nonsense, there was a certain amount of truth in it. Fran did seem impregnable, in every sense; and the fact that the other students kept their distance from her meant that she and I could spend all the more time together. There must have been something in me, the very opposite of Fran, that appealed to her – but of course I was very different then.

I said to Fran, one late July evening, the kind of dead, London evening that still makes me think of the end of schooldays, of the beginning of life, of Ireland, of joy: 'I'm going tomorrow. I wish you could come.'

Fran was sitting on the floor of one of my temporary bedrooms. There was a sprigged quilt on the bed, I remember, with cigarette holes burnt in it: my mother must have lent it to one of her drunken friends. Tarty mirrors lined the walls – you could see yourself walking in and going out like a dog at a show.

'You're going?'

'Cliff Hold.' The name sounded particularly secure in a room like this. 'I'll ask Moura . . . she's so kind, Fran – and you'd like to come, wouldn't you? She's bound to say yes.'

That was how I saw myself at the time. The favoured daughter of the beautiful Moura. 'Everyone' knew me out there. At parties, when I helped to hand round the mayonnaise-with-everything snacks there were knowing smiles and suggestions that it was a waste of my time to go back to England at all. But Philip was still at University then. I had to have a semblance of something to do.

'Ireland.' Fran put her head on one side. Her black hair swung over her face. 'Well, I don't know.'

I felt hurt, which seldom happened with Fran. To be indifferent to Cliff Hold, even if you'd never been there, was intolerable. And Fran had seen the photographs, of the house from the fuchsia lane – the stone eagle-gates, the clipped peacocks of box, the door with its heavy ledge of overhanging stone. She'd seen the house from the sea, taken when Philip and I had been out in the boat. And from Dunane, the view of the staircase garden under the house, which was windowless that side, and looked like a continuation of rock. She'd been excited at the idea of a place like that – so foreign, that was what she'd said.

'I'd like to get to grips with Ireland.' (At this point Fran already had her new job in the editing rooms of the great American TV network in Portland Place. Situations, countries were like dates in a box, and she plucked at them with a two-pronged fork: are they oppressive/potentially revolutionary régimes? Then she edited the incoming footage accordingly.) I knew she'd never been to Ireland – but nor was she yet in a position to make films of her own. I saw her trying to make up her mind whether it was worth going over, finding a 'line' she'd like to pursue and coming back to persuade her bosses of the validity of a short documentary. She didn't know then, she could hardly guess, how much material would fall in her lap, and by way of life rather than research. She sat calmly back on her heels on the floor of my room and said, 'No, Minnie. It's a nice idea. But I have to go to Turkey. I have to get to grips with Turkey.'

So Fran didn't come to Cliff Hold. I couldn't have known then either, that five years later Fran would marry Gareth. She met him in New York and married him within a month. She didn't even answer the letter of congratulations I sent at the time of the wedding. But then I didn't mean the congratulations. It seemed to me ludicrous that Fran – whom I'd known, who belonged to my memories of a happy past – and Gareth, the younger brother of everything I'd lost, should meet three thousand miles away and fall in love. I sat at the lino-covered table – we were in North Kensington by then – and stared out at the plane tree just coming into leaf. The barks of the trees were green with winter and the small, lighter green leaves danced about them in the wind foolishly, like a conjuror's handkerchiefs.

'I'm not surprised,' my mother said. 'Gareth would. Think of all the money.'

My mother usually referred to any substantial sum as 'lovely money' so I felt glad to be let off that at least. The doorbell rang: we were expecting a pupil. But I said, in that slow voice which so exasperates my mother: 'I didn't know Fran was so rich as all that.'

Of course you did, my mother might have replied. There was the door to open, though, and mention of my faulty memory depresses her more than it does me. So the subject was abandoned, except for vague echoes of my mother saying, in that house in Belgravia where we lived when I was at film school, 'Your friend told me her name. Or rather I had to force it out of her in these days of Cool.' (And she'd snorted; she was 'amused', her cigarette drooped ash.) My mother said Fran's name was Alderton. They were rich, even I must know they were one of the richest families in the States. She could have told, anyway – Fran had something special about her – she'd guessed it all along.

I didn't want Fran's special quality to have to do with money, so I must have forgotten intentionally that the Aldertons had museums named after them, that they had estates anywhere you care to mention, that the New York house, which I'd visited late in that wonderful year I thought myself engaged to Philip, had maids and two chefs and silver boxes of cigarettes that seemed to fill up as soon as they were emptied. When my mother spoke of Fran I remembered only the bright late October morning, my excitement and Fran's as we went to her offices in the Upper East Side and she showed me her first independently-made film.

31

Afterwards, we went to SoHo and had a meal of frogs' legs and dark red wine. I see the meal, and the red-checked tablecloth, more clearly than the film, which had men's faces dried by sun and wind, blinking against the sun in turbans – I'm ashamed to say I don't even know which issue Fran was doing her in-depth exploration on.

That was the New York when Vietnam was still in the air and Dylan's songs still blew around corners and into boutiques, stuffy with incense and dope. In Greenwich Village the sound blasted into the old houses, into the lower-ground apartment where a friend of Fran's – he was known as J – was making the kind of revolutionary documentary Fran desperately wanted the network to emulate. She was still very young then.

'Don't you see, Minnie, it's all people need. To see how it all really is. Not to be told a pack of lies dressed up as objective truth.' Fran stressed the word 'object-ive' as if it were a word from Hell. 'Like what J does – piecing together, making his points with existing footage . . .'

J, who was squatting on the floor, looked up at us smiling – his fondest smile, of course, reserved for Fran. She was so lovely – the tall, all-American girl with a hint of Red Indian blue in her raven black hair. You could see Fran leading the wagons into the Wild West, quelling rebellions, rearing a huge family of sons. And J, surrounded by his footage of the corruption of American companies in Latin America, the colonization, brothelization as he put it, of islands in the Caribbean under American influence, his clips of torture in the Philippines, was all the more amused and fascinated because Fran was so rich. It would have been unkind to discuss with her the nature of the régimes which her family, by way of investment,

32

supported or at least condoned. But it was the old story: Fran thought she could use her money – when she eventually came into it – to make the world a better place. Whether these people ever do is another matter. But I don't know about such things. I felt shy then, of J's admiring glances at Fran; surely he couldn't, too, for revolutionary purposes, be planning to use her money? Marry her, perhaps?

But if he was, Fran was obviously unaware of it. It came to me, as we walked out into decrepit streets loud with wailing music that Fran was very good at not noticing the attentions of men. They were, perhaps, irrelevant to her. We passed a huddle of shops and started to look for a cab (Fran always took cabs; she said with pride that they came off expenses at her job, but I shouldn't think any Alderton has spent much time on public transport). I told her I thought J's film-making methods very interesting. Fran hailed a cab at last; we settled.

'But what do you think of J?' I asked. We went at a rattling speed away from poverty, revolution, song, to the quiet streets of money: magnolia and wisteria outside the door.

'What do I think of him?' Fran looked at me in surprise. 'I told you, Minnie. That's the way to get the truth across. It's the only way.'

The cab stopped outside Fran's parents' house and we climbed out. I didn't think, until we were half-way through one of those 'simple' elaborate lunches Fran's mother used to lay on for us, that Fran hadn't answered my question about J. Or was she really like that, able only to see a person by their work or function? If she was, then Gareth, trained in Hugo's mould, was certainly Comrade Right. Or so I thought in the North Kensington flat when I saw the announcement of Fran's engagement – and I remembered the *oeufs en gelée* and Fran's mother holding a cigarette over a silver ashtray, and a dark brown light in the room, the colour of the chic hessian walls – and I remembered Fran saying to her mother: 'Minnie's getting married in the spring, Ma.'

Mrs Alderton turned to me: she seemed slightly surprised.

'I'll be living in Ireland,' I said. And then I had to describe Cliff Hold as best I could, and all along Fran and her mother looked, or so I suddenly thought, embarrassed by my descriptions, as if I were a savage, a person telling of something unimaginably far away. Yet why? God knows the country round Cliff Hold was crawling with rich Americans, as Hugo knew so well.

'We don't really like it there,' Mrs Alderton said when I had finally come to a halt.

So I said to my mother, when I heard the news of Gareth and Fran meeting and deciding to marry (and I'd seen my mother's cruel pleasure at my face – she knew those feelings of powerlessness well), 'Fran's family won't like this.'

'What do you mean?' My mother, who judged people by their homes and possessions, narrowed her eyes in happiness.

'It's because the Pierces haven't any money?' she said.

'No. It's not that.' I enjoyed her frown of impatience. I went to the door and pressed the buzzer; a pupil was on the way up.

'What then?'

But I couldn't supply a reason. I just remembered the prejudice, strong to me even after all that time. My mother looked furious. I went into the bedroom, as I did so often in the history of my life with my mother,

34

and sat on a chintz-covered bed and began to cry. And it wasn't until the worst of the crying was over that I thought of Fran and Moura – and gaped at the thought of them together. Then I thought of Fran happy at Cliff Hold and I began to cry again. But as it happened, although Hugo and Moura went out (twice, I think) to America to visit Gareth and their new daughter-in-law, Fran, until two days after Hugo was buried, had never visited Cliff Hold at all.

4

A light that's sharper than midsummer has come down over Dunane. Just as the tourists leave and the single men crowd in at Ryan's bar to stave off the gloom of winter ahead, the sun appears with a new brilliance, infusing the fields with a bright green: they look as if they've been painted on glass. The caravans, abandoned now, stand in the fields like shining toys. Up at Cliff Hold, the clipped peacocks of box are the only green that show the time of the year – a long, tiring summer has drained most of the life from them.

In this light, the Guards throw long shadows on the grass by the eagle gates. They stand back, deferential, for Moura to go in. They look up at the house – they were probably last here when they were boys, after throwing lines for lobsters in the sea under the rocks and scrambling up the path to see if Mrs Pierce would buy. They might have been asked in at Christmas by Moura's old cousins, who used to give bun-and-lemonade parties in rooms that then were bare and cold. I wonder, do they have memories like I do of this strange house that rises sheer out of rock at the end of the cliff? That's the kind of thought to keep away the other thoughts – of wondering, in terrible apprehension, what it is they've come to say.

Surprisingly, I'm waved through to the front door first. No good hanging back, trying to hear what they're saying to Moura. Turning, in the hall by Moura's flower basket and old boots and a bundle of hanging shapeless coats, I'm cheated of the news. Except that the Guards don't seem to be saying anything to Moura. They're silent; are they ill at ease? Why should they be? They're looking around, up at the windows of the house again.

I walked along the mosaic passage to the kitchen. That's where I am, under the clock, standing by the table with Moura's bric-à-brac, the mementoes her sons send back to her from another life.

Here it is. I pull out the photograph in the silver frame that no one's thought to polish, and Lily certainly never will. The photograph – is it the appearance of the Guards outside which makes me remember it? Their shadows, the strong black and white of their faces and uniforms like this photograph of Gareth and Fran's wedding day, under maple leaves that are black in the photograph taken in New Hampshire. Fran is wearing an antique lace dress. Her veil lies lightly on the long, black hair. She is exactly the same height as Gareth, who is wearing a real old-fashioned wedding outfit, suit and shirt and diamond studs and all. Well, I suppose the days of revolution are over – the 1970s were into their second half then – and he wouldn't want to displease the Aldertons.

The picture of Fran falls into my hand, and I can see her as she crosses Central Park from her offices. She is carrying the news of Hugo's death. It would be Fran who hears of it first: she deals with death in the news, after all, exclusively. (Poor Gareth, with his third-director job on feature movies, is far from the excitement of the real world, he's stuck in a web of imagined situations when Fran has all the real ones.) I see her walking under trees in Central Park. She looks tense. She arrives at the apartment. She walks up some stairs carpeted in dark blue. She lets herself into the apartment, where Gareth is sitting watching TV, a scribbling pad on his lap. He's pretending to work. Storyline. Concept. Script development. Fran puts her hands down on his shoulders, like they do on TV.

Footsteps in the passage, and voices. At last. But no, they're only the polite murmurs of the Guards asking the way. Gareth coughs, in the room down at the end of the passage where it turns to the left.

'The kitchen's along there,' Moura says. I can hear her quite distinctly now.

I stare down at Gareth's face, on the other side of the photograph in the old frame that cuts him off at the shoulder. But only Fran's voice returns to me.

'I heard some bad news today, Gareth. Hugo's been found dead. In some woods somewhere – well, you would know.'

Moura appears in the doorway of the kitchen. The Guards are behind her. They still look ill at ease and too good-mannered, like guests on an unwished-for tour of the house.

'Hugo's dead,' Fran says. (I can see they haven't noticed me, their eyes are on Moura as if silently pleading with her to help them tell her the terrible news.) But . . . what if Moura, who was happy today, who smiled in her tropical garden above the sea, suddenly smiles? I hope and pray she won't.

'We'd like to see everyone here,' the Guard says. 'In

37

particular, Mrs Pierce, we're looking for . . . er . . .
your son, Mr Gareth Pierce. Can you help us in this?'

Moura turned to me with the same baffled, mock-
ingenuous expression she'd used on the beach when
the Guards came up. As if on cue, Gareth coughed
again in his distant room. Moura smiled – the look of
triumph went so quickly I could swear the Guards
never saw it. A brave widow's smile replaced it.

'Gareth's in bed with a bad cold,' she said. 'But
I haven't seen Fran. We were just saying, weren't
we, Minnie? Where on earth can Fran have decided to
go?'

5

The plane landed at Cork airport. I walked past the
stewardess, who had a foxy face under a green hat
squashed sideways, and went out on to tarmac under
that heavy sky. I knew Moura would be there, waiting. I could hardly believe the mixture of strangeness
and familiarity in the small airport hall – the man
leaning against the exchange desk and talking, talking:
that low, unceasing voice as near to me as yesterday:
and the fact I'd forgotten I'd have to change my few
remaining pounds for exotic notes. Even as I did so, I
knew the transaction was simply a token: as always
with the Pierces, I would be entirely their guest,
entirely supported by them. At Cliff Hold, you never
saw money anyway. Shopkeepers in Dunane sent their
accounts to Hugo, who wrote out the cheques, pre-

sumably, in the study where he wrote his books.

The Pierces. It was the first time since my flight from my mother's flat that I'd taken in that there would be no Hugo-and-Moura at Cliff Hold. Only Moura – looking as untouched, as childlike, as if she'd never married at all. That's how she looked to me, at least, as I came out of the building with my bag: she was rushing towards me from the car park: as usual, she must have left the drive to the airport just a little late. 'Darling.'

I held back, as I always used to at first, from the brush of the dry cheek, the glimpse of a chin like Philip's. Then I kissed her. 'I can't believe it yet,' I said.

'No.' Again I tried to take in what had happened. I imagined Hugo walking in the woods. But he hated going for walks. What was he doing there? Moura must have been with him: sometimes she made him come on her painting expeditions, for his health. But no: she said he'd spoken to her as he left the house. I saw him stumbling in a long root of a tree, going headlong in dead beech leaves.

'He said, "I'll see you later, whenever that may be".' Moura's hands trembled on the wheel. We were crossing the Blackwater: the river lay silver under a leaden sky. Between banks with trees were white houses, some with fancy turrets like cut-outs in a cardboard theatre. When we got to the other side, I said to Moura: 'But what's odd about that?' It occurred to me that the shock of the accident might have driven her slightly mad. I thought, I must look after her well at Cliff Hold. That was what she'd asked me for, after all: she knew she needed help.

'Oh never mind,' Moura said. She sounded disappointed. Then she tried again: 'He didn't normally say that kind of thing. He was extraordinary about

39

time, don't you remember? If he said it would take him fifty-five minutes to finish a page he was writing, he finished it fifty-five minutes later. Or if he . . . if he was going down to the bar . . . and said he'd be forty minutes . . . he always was, although he didn't even own a watch . . . surely, Minnie . . . '

The effort of the memories was like forcing open the door of a cellar. I saw Hugo on his way down the fuchsia lane to the bar. He said, I'll be back in forty minutes. He carried the forty minutes in him, as he walked down past the sea birds and the row of white houses each one a step higher than the last, like stacked shoe boxes. In Ryan's he might drink with the old young men from the lonely farms – he might laugh or tell one of his famous stories, but he knew when it was forty minutes and time to go. It was extraordinary – he'd suddenly not be there – but no one in Ryan's could feel slighted. For Hugo had always just finished his pint, so that only a swirl of Guinness was left at the rim; and he had always finished his story too, walking away on a punchline that left another swirl, of laughter and pleasure, in the black of Ryan's Bar. It was one of Hugo's greatest qualities, this sense of timing. It was as if his life was ruled by a series of secret deadlines and he fitted and expanded his hours and actions to meet them. The sound of his step after exactly forty minutes brought action in the house too: another episode was to begin: Lily went to the oven door and out came the pie.

I took another look at Moura and then at the road. I said, 'Of course I remember, Moura. No, he never lost sight of the time.'

Silence fell between us as we started to climb towards Dunane. The river lay below and I stared down at the great bend of the Blackwater as it wound on to the west, to the edge of Blackstone, the house where

Moura grew up. I turned again to Moura and said: 'How's the old house – I mean, are Cousin Henry and Cousin Ottoline still there?'

Moura hardly bothered to reply, she nodded slightly. Of course, her cousins were no relations of mine. But as I hadn't said their names, or thought of their faces in the gloomy old house since the time I'd been – so nearly – the family, I was surprised at the way the names came out so naturally. And it occurred to me that I'd been summoned like a daughter, a daughter who's been away a long time, as happens in the west of Ireland when girls go to London or New York and come back embarrassed at the family meeting at the airport.

I said, but more for something to say, than meaning it, 'Do you believe . . . when you said Hugo said he'd see you later – whenever that might be – I mean, d'you think he had some kind of premonition?'

We reached the top of the hill. The Blackwater was hidden, it belonged to another world, a world of lowness and greenness and trees dark with the end of summer. And there, laid out in front of us, was the sea. As I'd always done, from the first school holiday that my mother took me to Cliff Hold, I gasped and wound the car window down. The sea was brown today, topped with vicious waves. I felt the old vertigo – the sway, the sickness, at the size of the waves as they attacked the cliffs this side of Dunane.

'Hugo didn't have second sight,' Moura said. She showed no interest in the sea, but then she lives right over it, in her room at the end of the house. 'If anyone is given to premonitions, surely it would be me,' she added with a faint smile, as if she found it strange to have to remind so close a relative of who and what she was. And I had a sudden memory of chill.

It seemed so long ago – and as far away as that part

of childhood which believes in witches, and spells that can summon a century of sleep or a walk over seven ranges of mountains in iron shoes. Yet Moura had taught us all to believe it – it was family lore – that her mother, that strong, wise, beautiful woman who lived at Blackstone – had been a possessor of the 'eye'. People were afraid to cross her. Moura said it was because she had magic powers. And Hugo laughed – and Philip and Gareth laughed – but I thought they all believed it, really. 'Moura has inherited her mother's magic,' Hugo would say, and throw her a pleased, funny look. We didn't know what he meant – was it just that Moura was so charming, so 'magically' different from other people? Or had she inherited this 'eye'? It used to frighten me, thinking of it. And I tried to remember Moura's mother at Blackstone – I thought I could see her on the high, dusty-smelling velvet seat by the window, looking out. A flat field with buttercups lay beyond the garden. Her eyes looked out on the swampy field, and the river. And I felt the chill again. But it must have been the cold from the sea, that I felt, for we were going down now, on the cliff road towards Dunane. The car slowed, held up by a removals van in front. Moura said, 'We need some petrol, Minnie. I'll just pull in here,' and as we waited by the pump I knew the moment to ask her what Hugo had meant was gone. The attendant, young, black-curly-haired, would have been a boy of ten when I was last here. And I only wondered later, when we'd pulled in to the drive at Cliff Hold, whether Moura was asking me, in her oblique way, to take in something I didn't know.

Much later, we sat in the dining-room dark with candles and their shadows on the dark walls, and I realized Moura hadn't once asked me about myself – how I was after all these years, how was my mother even, ordinary talk. But then she was in shock: even her voice was unlike her, I thought, high and unchanging. She said, picking at the food she never ate, 'Gareth's coming tonight, Minnie. In time for tomorrow, for the funeral.'

There would be nothing more to say of what it was like to arrive at Cliff Hold – nothing that wasn't a strange kind of replay of a decade before, down to the orange cats, several generations on, fighting still on the lawn by the gate – if Moura hadn't had to brake the car suddenly as we were climbing the last stretch of hill: brake so suddenly that we were thrown forward almost as far as the windscreen and then thrown back again. The car stopped altogether. Moura, who never swears, set her lips and stared out at the road. There was a rattling sound, then silence. We were on the cliff road, by the side of the shoe-box houses. In the quiet, the sea made a slapping sound against the sea wall. 'What was that, Moura?'

Moura tried the engine again. With a groan – the car seemed very old (I didn't recognize it, but perhaps it was another thing erased by the years and was in fact the car she'd always had) – we started and began to crawl upwards. Cliff Hold looks its most mysterious and rock-like at this point. But I'd seen the figure that darted out from the second shoe-box house, so close to the car's bonnet that Moura had had to stamp on the brakes. I felt the near-brush of the man's body, as if we could really have been on the point of running him down. My longings for the sentimental reunion with Cliff Hold disappeared; and I turned instead and stared back at the row of white houses as we went up the hill.

'One of the Rooneys.' Moura was bent forward over the wheel, as if she were trying to get away from the scene at greater speed than the car could afford.

'They've always been here.' Her voice was dry. 'Don't you remember, Minnie?'

I wondered if my memory, in which I thought I had so exquisitely preserved Cliff Hold, wasn't as much at fault as the rest of me. My mother, who disliked my 'haziness', as she called it, would be delighted to find that even Cliff Hold was half forgotten. 'The Rooneys,' I said.

'There are two brothers. One of them . . . comes to visit. The other lives here.'

'But which one was that?' I was so surprised by Moura's casual tone that I found myself pretending nothing had happened. Did Moura refuse to realize we had nearly killed a man? Was it possible that Moura and her world lived as they'd always lived, as untouched by the war in their country as if a bit of local poaching was all that ever went wrong? I remembered Moura's stories of how her mother had helped the Republican cause – how she'd made over her house in Dublin to a hospital, had been a friend of Maud Gonne – that I did remember. (And Hugo's embellishing of the stories, to divert himself because he'd heard them so often before. 'Moura's mother dressed up as a man, of course . . . she carried arms.' I saw Hugo again with force. And the American visitors, well drunk on claret and Gaelic coffee, laughing, waiting for the punchline they knew so well. 'She grew a beard,' Hugo said. 'It's the main danger of transvestism. Auto-suggestive. She was asked to join the circus and had to explain who she was.')

'That was the elder one,' Moura said.

And then I turned round again. We were at the gates to Cliff Hold. The shadowy figure had no doubt slipped down to Ryan's by the sea path, to take a few drinks after the experience of running in front of Moura's car.

44

I didn't ask about the Rooneys again. The car turned into the eagle gates, and I saw how much the peacock hedges had grown, and there were the orange cats still spitting under the window ledge of Hugo's room. I rushed headlong into the past. And in my rush I stumbled slightly on the shallow, worn doorstep and put my arm out – and there was Lily, looking just the same as she always has, with the same kirby-grip in her hair and the same sharp look in her eyes.

'Watch where you're going for God's sake, Minnie.' But Lily was laughing. She was pleased to see me: I could tell. Moura got out of the car. She said, as if she were miles from me and Lily kissing and hugging there in the doorway:

'Let's have tea in the drawing-room, Lily. Did you unwrap that cake?'

6

What does time do? And we can't even see it. There was a sense in that first evening at Cliff Hold of a September evening of ten years ago ripped from its grave and laid out in front of me like a preposterous joke. Or was it just because it was that kind of evening, quiet after the commotion of the waves – familiar and still, more like a memory than what is happening now? The 'sameness' hung over the house, and the trees outside, and over the bay; and I felt as I walked from room to garden to kitchen and back again, that the sameness was somehow false, as if a coat of varnish had been sprayed over the whole scene. Even Lily, after the greetings were over and she'd gone back to the kitchen, looked like a figure in an interior, embalmed in her white overalls and surrounded by all her sacred things. She was chopping herbs on a board. The smell of the herbs took me sharply back to the corner of the garden where Moura had years ago made a small patch for vegetables. Then I had to remember I wasn't smelling the herbs in my mother's kitchen in North Kensington and being transported over the years to Cliff Hold. I was actually here. The realization made me suddenly afraid: what happens if you walk into your own memory?

'You aren't usually here so late, Lily,' I said. I knew as I spoke that Lily did sometimes stay late – if Moura had a big party, or, when the boys were young, if one of them was ill. But nearly always she'd bicycle back to Ballinstrae, the village behind Blackstone where she lived with her brother Old Tom. Old Tom – the only companion she'd ever had. He'd been dependent on Lily since he was a child: there was something 'not quite right', as Moura put it, with Old Tom. Seven miles – a wobbling wheel – nothing would make her stay overnight away from him. Lily didn't look up and I tried again. 'Lily,' I said, 'tell me about Hugo. Was . . . he very ill? I mean . . . '

(My mother's words as I tried to pack a bag in my room in the flat. 'It was his heart. Poor Hugo. I always knew he had a bad heart.' And her slight, satisfied smile, which I knew meant that things were working out as my mother expected them to do: if you were happy, as Moura and Hugo undoubtedly had been, life would punish you severely for it. 'He wasn't so very old after all,' my mother said. 'Now let me see . . . ')

'There.' Lily said as if she hadn't heard me. She stooped: lamb cutlets came out of the fridge: the herbs

46

were pressed down into them and scattered into a green salad. There were six cutlets, clumsily hacked by the butcher in Dunane.

'Is Gareth going to be here for dinner?' I said.

The sameness was beginning to grip me now. I willed Lily to do something different – anything. As the feeling ebbed I knew it was useless: impossible to imagine Lily not being always the same. All those evenings we'd waited for Gareth to come back from school, the first day of the holidays from the English boarding-school, the boat at Cork met by Moura wearing an anxious-mother expression although in fact her mind was miles away, on her most recent paintings, or on the trip to the West that had inspired some of her most spiritual work. All those evenings Lily and I had waited in the kitchen by the white plate with six cutlets. 'I won't put them under the grill until I hear the car,' Lily always said. (The cutlets were Moura's idea of a treat: she envisaged something delicate, like a restaurant in Dublin or London. The Dunane butcher made uneven lumps with fat running right down the bone.)

'I'm not sure what time he's coming,' Lily said. 'But I won't put them under the grill until I hear the car.'

'But Lily – suppose the plane's late.' I had to prove to myself that Lily knew time was passing; that she knew Gareth was coming in a plane from New York and not by ferry or train from an English boarding-school. Gareth the married man – despite the wedding photo on the cabinet in the kitchen, I was still incapable of visualizing Gareth as fully grown-up.

'It won't matter how late he is,' Lily said. 'I'm staying the night.'

Something different, after all. And yet when it came I resisted it fiercely. 'But Lily, you hardly ever spend the night,' I said. I sounded like a child myself, I knew.

I thought of an adult reason for my obvious dismay. 'I mean, now I'm here I can look after Moura. You always like to get home, don't you, Lily.'

'I'm staying,' Lily said. 'Don't you worry your head about it, Minnie.'

The cutlets went into the grill pan but the gas stayed unlit. A French dressing, doubtless made earlier by Moura, was taken from the fridge and placed in a jug by the side of the salad. It was as if the meal, like the house and the evening, was preparing for future preservation. Lily turned to face me, as she always did when her most pressing work was done. She folded her arms over her thin body in the white overall. 'Mr Hugo was very ill, Minnie,' she said.

I don't know why I had to walk out of the house then and down through the garden to the sea; then along the side of the sea wall; then out suddenly into the rain-washed square at the end of Dunane where the fourth side is the sea. It was like running a thread in the elaborate walls of a maze. Somewhere, on the worn cliff path or on the step with half the front still bitten out – somewhere in the loop-shaped walk that makes up Cliff Hold and the fuchsia lane – and the drop to rocks and weed at high tide, sand cold and puckered when the sea is out, the scramble up the cliff again – there lies me, my childhood, my past. Round and round. A boomerang throw, that skims the fresh early mornings, and the dull afternoons when it looked as if the sea would never move; and the lights coming on in the house, so red, so exciting from outside, when you were safe climbing home up the rocks. Lights red in Hugo's study; Moura sitting under a white light in the sitting-room, stitching a cushion cover of flowers with spiky leaves.

Perhaps I was trying to walk myself into an understanding of the new reality, trace over the old paths

48

and lanes; but when you come to the house, the picture begins to fade. The red lights aren't on. Hugo isn't there.

Moura's car was in the main street of Dunane, parked outside Ryan's store. I walked self-consciously past. But why should anyone in the street know me now? If they did recognize Minnie, the girl who nearly married Philip Pierce up at Cliff Hold, they wouldn't find it particularly interesting: mine wasn't a story of emigration, success. I passed a girl with red hair and a tilting nose that I knew – I could have sworn I'd know it anywhere – but she walked by without a glance. Of course! She'd be a woman with a push-chair now, my red-haired girl. I walked like a ghost in the Dunane main street. On the pavements, men with yeasty faces walked in single file to the mock-ancient darkness of the bar.

The bus from Cork was late. An instinctive knowledge, that: the grey sides of the bus coming into view by the gas station at the end of the street; the glance at the clock over the bank. Four thirty-eight. The bus stopped outside Ryan's, doors rubbered open to spill out girls in tasselled hats. Across the road, I stood watching. The driver was expecting to pick up an order from Ryan's. And Mr Ryan's son – so tall now, as thin and pale as the ham his father slices all day long in the back of the shop – comes out and hands over a carton: eggs, toilet paper, frozen food in grey edifices of *Cork Examiner*. I half stepped forward. But the girls were crossing; and a car came; and there was a hooting and shouting –

'That'll be to drop at the Mayor's,' the boy had to say twice over the commotion. 'And wait, will you, while I go back for the spirits.'

The girls pushed past me on the pavement. I crossed at last. I stood looking up at the driver, open-

49

mouthed, like a passenger who's lost her way, or is not 'quite there' – as if I wanted to go away but lacked the means.

'You'll need spirits here, then,' the driver laughed at the receding back of the boy. He frowned down at me, noticing me for the first time. What did I want? Did I know what I was about to hear?

The boy turned in the shop doorway, grinned and made a V-sign.

'Anything new on the Ardo killing, then?' the driver called, suddenly curious, tired of his jokes about spirits. 'Hey, what do they say?'

But the boy had gone into the shop: the bright, packaged goods had swallowed him up and only the top of a carroty head was visible over the display of cans, each with a salmon lying still among weeds. The driver shrugged. I walked away – before Moura could come out of the shop – before I could stop and listen for more. I walked – but not in the loop of the lane up to Cliff Hold. I went back the way I'd come, along the beach and up the staircase garden from the sea. The cast of memory was broken: I had to look down carefully to see where I could put my feet.

Moura came in. She'd had to go into Dunane to get something forgotten on an earlier trip – she was absent-minded to the degree that Mrs Ryan in the store kept her own list of what Cliff Hold might be running out of at any given time. This time it was butter. She laid down the green-emblazoned packets on the top of the cabinet and stood back with a satisfied expression, like someone who has found a precious object after much searching.

'Shall I put on the cutlets?' Lily said.

'Moura,' I said, 'is Gareth coming in time for dinner? When you went out now I thought you'd gone to the airport to fetch him.'

Moura glanced at me and then away again. Already I was like someone who was a permanent fixture at Cliff Hold – we'd had tea in virtual silence, even, like members of a family with no need to speak to each other. Moura wouldn't speak of Hugo, or of his death: it was as if my presence had brought her a nursery safety, a plunging back into the time when I had been there and she and Hugo had had many years behind them and many ahead, too. I had to repress a sudden feeling that the cutlets were for Moura and myself – and Hugo. But of course that couldn't be.

'Whatever time he comes he'll get his supper,' Lily said. 'It'll be a long drive from Shannon in the middle of the night.'

The gas went on after this. Lily must have thought she would wait for the sound of the car before she started cooking because she had indeed forgotten that Gareth was no longer coming from his English boarding-school. She was old. She was ten years older. Her memory was failing. For a moment, in that strange evening that was so exactly the same and yet so totally different from the past, Lily and Moura and I stood in silence in the kitchen and let the varnished light deepen round us. Then the fat on the Dunane cutlets started to sizzle. Lily moved with that deceptively young step to the rack of vegetables by the sink.

'Will I be putting in a baked potato for Mr Gareth?' she said. 'And I can put the meat in for him low.'

'What . . . oh, yes.' Moura had gone to the window, was staring out. The stillness was going: a small wind chased the ragged palms in the garden of rocky paths and steps hewn in stone. I'd already been down there, to revisit the bay at low tide, the puddles of weed and water where Philip and I had gone in up to the tops of our boots.

'There'll be no one awake to feed the poor boy if he

comes in the middle of the night,' Lily said. 'I could set the alarm and get up to feed him if you like, Mrs Pierce.'

'Oh come on, Lily.' Moura sounded all at once weary, exasperated to breaking point. 'Gareth's grown up now. Just leave it warm . . .'

'And he's not bringing his wife with him,' was Lily's reply as she turned the gas grill low over the spitting meat.

I followed Moura out into the garden. She pointed at new flowers and new shrubs that had grown thick and tall, planted since I last was there. We left the garden and walked along the cliff path, and at the point where you can stand back and see Cliff Hold, perversely open and welcoming to the Atlantic, cold and closed off to the village behind, we stopped and turned. The promontory is narrow here. I thought: this is where I'll ask about Hugo. Standing under the window where Moura sits and paints and where Hugo used to come in and place a hand on her shoulder when she was in deep concentration: standing at the nearest point to a death fall on to the rocks and the sea below.

'Moura,' I said.

'I want to show you my pictures,' Moura said. 'Shall we go in?'

'Yes,' I said. I always said yes, after all. 'But Moura . . . can't you . . . don't you want to talk about Hugo? How . . . how it happened?'

Moura slipped her arm through mine. When she did this there was no feeling of intimacy: the opposite rather, as of coming up gently against something fragile, inanimate, a piece of driftwood, perhaps, or a branch with dry leaves. Moura's thin arm and dry hand rested lightly in mine as we walked home.

'There's so much to say, Minnie darling. And nothing at the same time. At least you knew him well.

Remembering that gives me strength.'

How could I ask of the circumstances of Hugo's death? We went into the house by the long window on to the steeply sloping lawn from the drawing-room. In the half-light the leather armchair that was Hugo's favourite could have been full with his bulky, slumped figure. The bulk was cushions, of course – but I felt too aware of him there, listening to my foolish talk, to speak of him aloud. His head was on one side, and very heavy-looking, as if it were a parcel put down carelessly on his shoulders and about to topple off at any moment. His eyes, also heavy and very dark, stared out with an air of mock pomposity from the white marble mantelpiece, where I knew they were part of a garland design linking black and green and red stone in the surround. But they were his eyes. Just above the tall back of the chair, the absurdly lolling head still showed itself against the light now racing out as fast as the Dunane tide.

'I think I've found a new strength in my painting,' Moura said. She came further into the room and I thought she was going to go over and kiss Hugo's ghost. The light was a dark green now, the colour of yew or cypress. Moura stumbled against a small table. She righted herself, as she always did.

'Lily might have put on the lights,' she said in a cold voice. 'But I suppose she's not used to being here in the evening.'

Moura found a lamp. Under the tasselled fringe a light suddenly gleamed out. From the small table a pile of letters had been knocked to the ground. Moura stooped and picked them up, glanced at them once and slid them into the pocket of her dress. She would have to look after all the letters and bills now, I thought. Poor Moura.

'The pictures are in my room,' she said, leaving the

drawing-room a little too quickly, walking away from the grate where there was no point in lighting a fire without Hugo, going without looking back at the absolute emptiness of the chair now the light was on. 'If we can see our way up, that is.' And she gave a slight laugh, half affectionate, half pitying, which I knew was the sound she made when she thought of the defects of Lily. So I took my chance – if I couldn't talk of Hugo I could at least clear up one thing that didn't belong in this mirror of a summer evening ten years ago.

'Why is Lily staying here, Moura?' I said. 'She never used to, did she? Is her brother . . . Old Tom . . . ?'

'Yes, he's still alive.' The words made me wince. Moura groped for a switch in the hall. The passage opened up before us, and the stairs up to the rooms where Moura painted and slept. 'Lily's staying here for, well, for company,' Moura said as we climbed up to the landing with its familiar smell of oil paints and rose and lavender dried in bowls.

'Company?' But it was too late. We had gone into Moura's room. The last of the sea light came in through the casement window at the end. I'd seen her in my mind often enough sitting at that desk, the easel to one side, the expanse of sea stretching ahead.

'I'll show you the results of my last trip to Galway,' Moura said. 'Although it may look more like the moon.' And she shuffled canvases under the desk, her mouth set in thought, her eyes invisible in the dying light. 'There's one I want to show you before it gets completely dark. Ah, here it is.' A grey stonescape was held up, complete with the spiky thistles Moura loved to paint. It looked harder, stronger than her earlier work. But I was thinking, as Moura said she had to admit we needed the lamp to look at the rest of the pictures, of her use of the word 'company'. Had things, then, become dangerous in this part of the world after all? What was Lily protecting Moura from? Or was it the other way round? Surely I'd have known if things were frightening or dangerous here. It was completely alien to Moura ever to say she needed support, or even company. Moura liked to be alone. And Lily – old, frail Lily – she'd never missed a night at Blackstone with her brother Tom.

'I'm very happy you find the painting purer and simpler than when you were last here,' Moura said. 'That's just what I hoped you'd say. Shall we go down?'

It was always like that at Cliff Hold, the meals seemed to run into one another, and the appetite never flagged. Sea air, my mother used to say with some irritation when I returned to London plump and rosy. But one wouldn't want to live there all the time, she'd add. (This thought always seemed to make her feel better.) 'One would simply go out of one's mind.'

I had wanted to live there the whole time. That was the trouble. I watched Lily come in and put four cutlets on the hotplate and I watched her walk out again. I wondered if she carried a gun these days, to provide this famous 'company' – but the idea was ludicrous. I smiled. Moura had meant she needed Lily's company since losing Hugo – after all, she hadn't seen me for so long that we might have disliked each other on sight. It would have been too much of a risk to ask Lily to go home.

'What are you thinking about?' Moura said.

We'd taken the lumpy cutlets from the hotplate by the time she spoke and I was busy hacking at mine with an ancient and unsharp silver knife. The dining-room was very dark and the candles, made of wax as fat and lumpy as the fat on the Dunane meat, guttered in the wind that came in always in that house, in a multitude of windows and cracks and crevices and under doors. Their shadows went up on the walls, which were made even darker by a series of tapestries, hung close together.

'I was thinking how I'm looking forward to seeing Gareth,' I lied. I knew Moura knew that I was thinking of the mystery of Hugo's death and of Lily's presence at Cliff Hold. 'I mean, I can't imagine what he must be like by now.'

Moura stopped pretending she was trying to eat the cutlets and laid down her knife and fork. There was a bottle of white wine on the table between us and she poured us both a glass.

'Nor can I,' she said.

'What do you mean?' I looked at Moura lifting the thin-stemmed glass to her lips and her mouth puckering as she took a sip.

'What I mean,' Moura said, 'is that I haven't seen Gareth for four years.' For the first time she looked straight back at me. 'I shouldn't think you knew that.'

My first reaction was that she couldn't possibly be telling the truth. It was true, then, that the shock of Hugo's death, the dread of tomorrow's funeral, had muddled her mind and made her jump years, almost as I'd been doing since I arrived at Cliff Hold. I said in a quiet voice that sounded like an unconvincing imitation of a nurse: 'You must mean four months, Moura. Surely . . . I mean . . . he would have been over for Easter, wouldn't he?'

That's how I still saw the Pierces and their relations with their adoring sons: Easter and Summer and Christmas holidays at Cliff Hold. It came to me, with some discomfort, that I thought of Philip in that way too: it had all been just one long school term since we'd last seen each other: he'd appear any minute, with a new degree or an academic honour of some kind and Hugo would stride out of his study into the hall and slap him on the back.

'You can't mean that, Moura,' I said as I faced this new discomfort. I felt a blush going down the side of my face. Was this why I'd come so readily – to see Philip rather than comfort Moura?

'Four years,' Moura said. 'It's true.'

I thought: Philip was always favourite, but she worshipped Gareth too. How can this have been allowed to happen?

'We went to the wedding, of course,' Moura said. 'And to the States twice in the year or so after that. Then – well, it stopped.'

'But how?' I leaned forward to catch Moura's face behind the candles. I hardly noticed Lily come in, remove the half-eaten cutlets, make a sniffing sound and go out.

'It wasn't a question of not being able to afford it,' Moura said with another of those wry smiles which were new to her – whether since Hugo's fall or earlier I couldn't say. 'No. We even offered them the fare to come over here. Not that . . . she . . . needed it of course.'

'Fran.' I thought I'd better say the name. 'No, Fran doesn't need it. So . . .'

'She wouldn't come. She wouldn't let Gareth come either.'

I gazed at Moura as if she'd spoken in an unknown language. Those years in the flat with my mother – the Christmases when I'd pictured the Pierce family by the log fire in the sitting-room, Hugo stirring hot whiskey punch with a spoon. The pictures turned to slush like advertisements: all was false. Derisively, Easter church bells rang in my ears.

'Why?' Still, the sinking feeling kept on: I knew I

was really wondering: did Philip not come then? Is he coming now?

Moura shrugged. 'Always a good reason. Work. Fran makes films, you know.'

The word 'films' was said with absolute lack of interest. Only pictures counted for anything with Moura, of course. Especially Moura's pictures: sea, dry cliffs that looked as if they'd been scraped on the canvas with a palette knife. Hard blue or grey skies jabbed on with the same force.

'I knew Fran,' I said. 'I wondered if she'd told you that, when . . . when she and Gareth . . . met.'

'I think she did.' Moura looked bored. What had been an extraordinary coincidence for me had been hardly worth the notice for her. No doubt she thought 'everyone' knew each other in London, as they had in the days when she'd been young and known my mother there.

'I was so surprised,' I said, 'when she met . . . married . . .'

'It was a pity.' Moura rose and with a sharp breath blew out the candles. We groped our way out of the dining-room into the pebble-mosaic corridor. Moura guided me into the sitting-room. There was a fire by now, I saw, and signs of Lily: a newspaper folded by the side of Hugo's chair, a tray with water, whiskey and gin.

Moura sat down and picked up her embroidery bag. I sat at right angles to her and watched as she pulled out the sea colours she always used. The empty leather chair dominated us, with its fat cushion plumped out and uncreased.

There was the clock, making the kind of unwanted noise clocks make when a difficult silence falls. But I was glad for it. Without it we'd have had nothing but the sea, which was beginning to roar outside, as it so

58

often did on autumn evenings after a still day. Then Hugo would say, 'Days are drawing in, thank God!' And Moura would look up at him from the pale wools and say she always loved the light to last the whole evening through.

When I did speak and ask when Philip was coming, I heard Moura's needle in the silence go in and out of the canvas with a rough asthmatic scratch.

'He sent a cable,' Moura said. 'He's got to cover the summit meeting. Then he'll come.'

'But . . .'

'Hugo would have wanted him to do that,' Moura said quietly before I could make any clumsy remark. 'Minnie, could you get the coffee, my dear? I think Lily must have forgotten.'

I went into the kitchen stunned. I'd taken for granted, I suppose, that I'd see Philip and his absence struck me for the first time with force. I brushed up against the jumble of old tourist junk and gifts on the cabinet as you go in, and a dry gourd with rattling seeds (memento of Philip's trip to Mexico at the time of the collapse of the oil prices, Moura had said) tumbled to the ground. Lily woke with a moan: she'd been dozing by the side of the stove, guarding Gareth's cutlets and rock-like baked potato. I bent to retrieve the gourd and kicked it with my foot this time. A crescendo of dry, mocking music started up.

'The coffee,' I said. I picked up the tray and headed for the door. A small spoon with an enamelled handle tipped from the bowl and sugar spilled out on the tray. Then – why do these things happen –

'Minnie!'

Footsteps along the pebble-laid corridor. The sounds I'd been hearing magnified a thousand times: the soft rush of the curtains, the pounding of the sea that was like a bludgeon outside on the hard water, the crash of china, the spoons falling and tumbling like metalled, bright insects on the kitchen floor.

'She can't help it.' Moura's voice. The only sound that was almost inaudible, as far away as a voice in a far-off summer's day.

'She was slipping just now,' Lily said. 'I didn't know what to say, Mrs Pierce.'

'That's enough, Lily.'

'We'll put her in Mr Hugo's room then.'

'No, no, Lily. I told you to make up the visitors' room.'

'And if she's not well?'

'Lily. That's enough. All right, put her in there then.'

The voices died away. I was alone.

Then, round-faced and brown and plain, the kitchen clock: not like the gold clock over the marble mantelpiece in Moura's sitting-room, the gold clock with a pendulum like a gold necklace swinging on a white porcelain neck. Just the plain, loud ticking of the kitchen clock – and in between the beats, Hugo who was never late, walking between the minute hand and the second hand on the grimy face of the clock. Hugo walked into a thicket of Roman numerals and fell in the roots. He tripped, fell over and was dead.

When I woke it must have been about two in the morning. I was in Hugo's old dressing-room, across the passage from where Philip used to sleep when he was a boy. Lily had left the light on. Hugo never slept in this room but his clothes and papers lay messily here, the papers creeping in somehow from his study, from the sitting-room or the garden: he liked to have a bath and then stay in his towel, reading on the bed. I had never known anyone read as much as Hugo. Even in situations where there was nothing to read – trapped in the car, waiting for Moura to finish her erratic shopping – or at Ryan's bar if it was empty and there was no one to hear the tales of Acapulco and New York and Paris – of gangsters and hold-ups – of diamonds in cold-cream jars smuggled over East European frontiers – of old-school-tie spies who had confided their brilliant treachery to Hugo before defecting to Moscow – if the bar was empty and the sea lay outside in a slab of grey, as unwilling to listen as the peeling walls, then Hugo would read the beer mats, the racing page of an old *Cork Examiner* left last night down by the table leg. His eyes glinted with amusement at some item or classified ad. His endless punning mind played with the words until it was time to talk again.

I know now that I must have been woken by steps outside, but at the time I felt only happy to be awake, to be safe in this room. I must have slept deeply because it took some time to remember, in spite of the sight of Hugo's buff trousers folded over a chair and a pile of shirts (which Lily must have been sorting) on the floor, that Hugo was actually, irremediably dead.

In those minutes between sleep and waking, I remembered how Hugo and I went on the sea, in the boat he taught Philip and me to row; and how I sat beside him in the old car as we drove to Blackstone and then up to the hills at Ardo. We got out and stared, fascinated as always by the huge sweep of bright yellow cornfield and the black, ruined castle. Rooks, tall trees. 'Tell me again why it's haunted,' I said. (Hugo was the kind of man you could go on asking that kind of thing. He was never impatient with children.)

'The wicked owner was ambushed and shot,' Hugo said with a smile. The route was always the same: after standing by the edge of the corn, and staring at the castle and the black trees far the other side, and mock-shuddering in the air that never seemed to stir over Ardo, we got in the car and went down the narrow road to the cove and the sea. Philip and I ran in and out of the waves as the tide came in, dodging the fast tide that shot in as suddenly as a tongue of leather into a shoe.

'Why was he so wicked?' As we left, under a sky the colour of vinegar, I liked to look back once more at the castle and the trees and the rooks.

'He starved the peasants. He let them die. In the end, two brave men lay in wait for him in the big beech trees at the back. They killed him. They were hanged for their pains.'

Then I would see the two brave killers swinging from gibbets made high in the beech trees. The wicked landowner lay under them in a thick covering of beech leaves. Now Hugo was lying there too – but what had he done to harm anyone?

I knew by the time I was properly awake that Hugo wasn't lying there now, of course. But I couldn't picture him anywhere other than in the woods at Ardo. I stared round the room in a kind of despair, in bewilderment at the unexpectedness of things. In the Westerns Hugo had loved to take us to in the cinema in Cork, in the boyish adventure novels that were still his favourite reading – 'You can't beat old Bulldog Drummond . . . give me Henty or Ballantyne and I'll be happy for years on end' – there was a pattern of death and valour and revenge that made some sense. 'But it never did make sense, of course,' Hugo would say, laughing, after he'd said he'd go to the ends of the earth for a Kipling Jungle Tale or a chapter or two of a previously unknown Rider Haggard. 'It was British imperialism that laid down the rules: Britain was "She who must be Obeyed".' But he loved those books all the same, loved them in a simple, boyish way, just as

62

their authors would have wanted him to. He said once that the two spies he'd known, the public-school men who'd fled via the Middle East to Russian safety, had taken Sapper and Conan Doyle and Henty with them. Those were the thoughts I had over all the long years in London – when I was separated from the family, and the glamour of the Robin Hood/pirate/swashbuckling fun that Hugo made of himself for our entertainment. Yet when these thoughts came into my mind there was always, too, the memory of the betrayal – as my mother told it to me the summer I came back broken-hearted off the boat-train from Cork, 'Hugo would never have let Philip marry you, Minnie. He was far too ambitious for his son's future. Oh yes, Philip may have wanted to marry you – but Hugo would never let him marry a girl like you.'

All Hugo's books are in the big bookcase at the end of the bed. Will Philip get them now? The adventures of brave, simplehearted British heroes – the kind of adventure tales that seem to appeal to masters of betrayal and deviousness. These were useless thoughts, though, as I knew, lying there on the bed where Hugo had read and rested and scribbled his books in note form before shutting himself in the study to type them out. Useless because I'd loved Hugo and I still did. Well – everyone knew you couldn't help loving Hugo.

I got up and walked to the window. The curtain didn't need pulling back, there was already a chink at the side where I could look out. There were steps on the gravel outside. A car's lights made monsters of the clipped peacocks. The front door was lit up, and so was the upper floor of Cliff Hold, where only Moura and her paintings were allowed room. A suitcase dragged up to the step. And I was sure I heard Lily's voice – patient Lily, rewarded at last.

There was nothing I could do, though. They weren't expecting me to join them – not after the disastrous end to the evening in the kitchen. The steps went back over the gravel and the lights went out. It was quite dark suddenly – just a thin moon – and I saw myself as silly as a heroine in a romantic novel, standing in a nightdress by the window of an old house, looking out for a lover. When the footsteps came back from the car, I shrank behind the curtain. An invisible figure went past, disappeared into the hall. And I thought: I'm not one of the family. Not even for Hugo, in the end.

For if Hugo had had this cool, mocking eye towards the rest of humanity, his family was exempt from it. His family was sacred – if you didn't belong to it, in fact, you weren't safe and never would be. I couldn't understand, when Hugo had spent so much of his life attacking the 'institution of the family' (and had taught his sons to do the same) the holiness which had to surround his own particular family. If he believed in equality, surely, anyone else would be as important and valuable as a member of one's family? That used to make Hugo laugh, when we sat in his study talking late after Philip and I had come back from one of our fishing expeditions. Hugo liked to tell me I was naive and that he found it charming. It was as if I'd missed the whole point of life: you believed certain things on paper but it was accepted they were nothing like the truth in reality. I suppose my blankness in that whole area must have been because of the way I was brought up: my mother believed in nothing – except the gossip of the day. I stumbled through a C of E school without giving a thought to religion. Only as I grew up in the holidays at Cliff Hold did I glimpse this dichotomy – it felt like a fault, a vein of a different mineral from the rest running under the house – of strongly held, early self-indoctrinated beliefs, co-existing with their opposite, the soft silt of old customs and unquestioned reverence and love.

That Hugo did revere Moura was in no doubt. He'd had affairs with many women before – that was how my mother put it – but none had come anywhere near Moura. Her beauty, her reticence, the fierce egotistical energy that forced her to go out painting in all weathers and at all hours – even if guests were expected or someone important to Hugo, someone over from London or New York or California to talk to him about his books – this force that Moura had always quietly possessed, kept Hugo in her thrall. And the boys: they were hallowed by being the products of this special union. They were extensions, not as important as the union itself but as absolutely demanding of loyalty as one's own foot or hand, which one would hardly want to cut off (Hugo's way of putting it this time). Outsiders either marvelled or laughed at the closeness of the Pierce family. They seemed above and beyond ordinary people – they were above and beyond everyone but themselves. When they were young, Hugo taught the lesson of how to survive in, and eventually conquer the world.

So I wasn't surprised, somehow, when I sat crying in that North Kensington flat, to hear my mother say it had been Hugo who had dissuaded Philip from marrying me. After all, one of the first lessons he must have taught is that to have a remarkable wife – of good family probably, of some financial means certainly – is of paramount importance in the struggle against the evils of capitalism, the disappointments of communism etc. I would have been no support for Philip. To sustain him in these trials and disappointments, stand by him as he rose, entirely by his own efforts, to a position of irreproachable reputation, scourger of the infamous, famous himself for being that, would have been quite beyond me. At least, I was soon sure of it after that last summer at Cliff Hold. It was as if every object in the house turned against me, turned away from so maladroit and unsuitable a future wife.

It was Moura's compassion (a word Hugo said was suspect, a part of bourgeois hypocrisy – except he stopped using the word *bourgeois* after it became fashionable), Moura's sense of caring, then, that made her invite me to Cliff Hold the summer after Philip had flown off to the States. She was making a statement, I suppose: a person isn't expendable just because one member of the family decides not to marry them. More than that – if Hugo's loyalty to his family was strong, then Moura's was like something out of legend or myth: fierce in her protection of her sons, her love for her husband, her support of friends or dependants. And I was seen as a dependant as well as a friend. I'd spent too long at Cliff Hold not to be counted almost as one of the family. (Moura's sense of family was wider than Hugo's because her family came from that part of the world and had been there hundreds of years.) If anyone was wronged – or there was a farming dispute – or some kind of scandal involving the family, Moura acted swiftly, unerringly. She didn't mind the consequences. No member of her family – or Hugo's and his – was ever in the wrong. People were afraid to cross Moura – the rich because they knew she would stop at nothing and might drag their names through the mud; and the poor because the tales of Moura's mother and her powers of retribution still circulated in the neighbourhood of Ballinstrae and Dunane. So I knew – as I was so much a part of the family then, so accepted by Moura already – that it was Hugo who told Philip to leave for America while there was still time. Moura was unhappy for me: in the summer after Philip was gone, she made me go with her on her painting trips down the Western seaboard or set out to sea and put down lines for lobsters – only this time with her for company instead of Philip – and all the time I let her down with my moans of misery and self-pity. No wonder she didn't ask me again. She said, when I left, 'Minnie, I don't think this has done you any good. You must get on with your own life now.' But my own life was as firmly laid down at Cliff Hold by then as the thick, dry colours Moura stabs on to the canvas. I had to wait until now – until she really needed me again, to come back to the place I never really left.

How could I not have opened the door of Hugo's dressing-room that night and gone out into the passage, clutching myself in an old blue dressing-gown seized at the last moment from a chair by the tumble of books and papers that spilled over everything? The alternative, which was to lie in the dark and let the sea, and the boat with Philip, run aground in the woods at Ardo where the fallen figure of Hugo lay stranded on a woodland floor of waves and broken shells, was too grim, too repetitive. I walked quietly to the sitting-room door. My bare feet were cold on Moura's Roman design of pebbles in Pompeian garlands and baskets of flowers.

Hearing Gareth's voice was the first shock. I stood braced against the door jamb. Of course: it was as Philip had spoken when I last heard his voice. Gareth had then still had the half-strangled voice of adolescence. But I thought, it must be Philip in there. He's come after all. Of course he would – however much Hugo would have wanted him to do his important work in America, Philip would have insisted on coming over.

'Darling,' Moura was saying, 'you must be so tired.'

'Lily shouldn't have waited up for me,' the voice said.

'Yes, but she's so pleased to see you. I mean – it's such an age . . . '

'Oh I know, Moura. I know.'

A silence. I saw Philip in the stern of the boat while I rowed, in Dunane Bay that was that day as flat as glass. 'We will get married, won't we, Minnie?' he said. 'We'll have a pact. If one of us goes away we won't say goodbye.'

'Lily was looking better than I'd expected,' the voice came from the sitting-room. 'Does she still cycle back to Blackstone every night?'

'Oh yes.' Moura's voice, sounding bored and impatient. She wanted to talk about what had happened, of course, but the boys' upbringing in the English public school had made them over-reserved.

In the boat, Philip said, 'We won't say goodbye unless we really mean it. When we know we're going to be . . . together . . . again we'll just say *Addio*. In front of strangers, anyway.' He meant in front of grown-ups but was too old by then to admit it. How we enjoyed using it, though, when we parted at the end of the holidays – *Addio*, Philip, *Addio*.

I missed some of the conversation in the sitting-room standing like that at the door, dreaming of Philip. Then the voice said, 'But Lily can go home tomorrow night, Moura, surely? Now I'm here, I mean.'

'It's all right, Gareth. Don't worry.'

Of course it had to be Gareth all along. But it's strange what putting the wrong face to a voice can do. Philip disappeared. Gareth was faceless to me. The

68

realization of this came like a shot of panic, in the passage where I stood illicitly, cowering in the dark and framed by the etching of light round the door.

'I need Lily here,' Moura said. 'And Minnie's here, Gareth, I didn't tell you. She rang and I asked her to come. She was in London.'

'Who's Minnie?' Gareth said.

7

When I look back to the day of the funeral, two things stand out. Maybe it'll be different when there's more time between then and now – or maybe it won't – it'll be stuck, preserved, like those summers ten years ago that have slid into the present like shuffled cards. From here and now the day is a chasm, dark and deep and with two sides that only occasionally are bridged, by a slender bridge that turns out at a change in the weather to have been nothing more than a trick of light. One side is the dark morning, heavy with rain, and the dark cars low on the road. The other side is the evening – laughter and firelight and song – this is how Hugo would have wanted it: a party, a party, never a wake. Balloons in the hall, like the Christmases of the past. Between the two hangs the quickly-snapped thread of reason and explanation: voices whispering, faint flashes of the truth.

The funeral attracted a large crowd. Of course Hugo's funeral would – but there's something so private, so removed from the world of publicity or fame about Cliff Hold that it still came as a shock to see the TV cameras by the gates of Dunane Protestant church – and the flashlights, which made Moura lower her head – and the journalists from Sweden and France and Belgium and the United States and England. And the inhabitants of Dunane too, standing by the railings and staring at Moura as if they'd never seen her before in their lives, as if grief had put her in a country infinitely further away than any of those represented by the journalists or dignitaries inside the church. But Moura didn't look back at them. The glare of lights was an affront to the mourning the dark day had pulled on. Moura would never wear sunglasses. So only her stooped head was visible; and she walks usually so upright, with head erect and a short neck strongly planted on her shoulders.

Gareth and Moura and I had all gone down from Cliff Hold in one car. Gareth was pale and tired after his long journey in the night and didn't say anything. I wondered if he and Moura had sat up much longer, after I'd crept back to bed in shame at my eavesdropping. They must have, surely. I felt secrets between them as I sat awkwardly on the tip-up seat, facing their white faces and the receding view of Cliff Hold in the rear window. I thought of the strained breakfast, when Gareth tried too hard to show how well he remembered me. By the time Cliff Hold had lost its open side and was no more than a rough wall rising out of a rock from the sea, a staircase of flowers rising from the base, I longed to run out of the slow car and disappear along the cliff. The bond that held Moura and Gareth after all the years of his absence was too strong to be intruded on. We went at the speed of a snail along the lane, the coffin in the first car pointing straight downhill to Ryan's Bar.

If I'd been more detached, cooler in the presence of

emotions from which I was necessarily left out (what is the value of your grief after ten years?) I would have seen then what recorded itself only in the brain's eye for examination later. I would have looked sharply at Moura and Gareth, to see if they had seen, from their deep seat facing the front, the sudden movement by the line of white houses near the sea wall, the houses that go up like steps, with people living, or so it looks, in the earth under each step. I didn't though. I stayed with my eyes on the small window behind Moura and Gareth's heads, staring unwaveringly like a child in front of a TV set. Very slowly, because of the excruciating speed of the car, the picture grew smaller. Only when we turned at the bottom of the hill into the main street did it shrink to pin-size and disappear. I thought of the two men – and the old woman with white hair – standing on the doorstep of the white house. I thought of the larger of the two men, lurching out in our path. After the man had fallen back, and as I was remembering, or trying to remember the lunging, stoutish figure of the man the day before, feeling the near-thud of his body under Moura's car – a young woman came out of the house and stood beside the white-haired woman on the step. She had on a black sweater, very tight, and a black pencil skirt. Then the car turned ponderously into the main street. We swayed slightly in our seats at the turning and the picture was gone.

The church. Editors, mayors, the castle-owning aristocracy old and new – and in the back pews a sprinkling of local farmers, the sad bachelors saved by Hugo with his jokes from a morose depression that lasted as long as winter, the season when there are no tourists to bring hope to Dunane. They were the ones who looked round when we walked up the aisle, with the same look of frank curiosity as the other inhabitants of Dunane who stood at the railings of the old churchyard. Did they think highly of Hugo when he was alive? Or were they there because there was little else to do on such a dark morning and the bar at Ryan's might suddenly feel chilly without Hugo coming down the lane to pass his forty minutes flat? Did they feel Hugo had become almost one of them? Or were they willing to play along with his own delighted fantasy that he was Irish to the core, a rebel and a romantic who was entirely on their side?

But what was their side? I'd been too long away to know what these ageing young men, victims of decline, of their own inertia in the face of parental pressure, when it came to emigration, actually felt about the happenings in their country now. The troubles began about the time I left – and Hugo, then, had given out his usual speech, of hatred of the British, of furious contempt for the arrogance and negligence that marked all their dealings with the poor, the colonized. Had he modified his views, come to see both sides of the question? It seemed unlikely. He had treated the violence in the end as he always did: a 'riotously funny' novel where the 'Irish question' takes over the world and blows us, eventually, to smithereens. ('A little too black for me,' my mother had said when she gave it back to the library.)

I slid into the pew behind Gareth and Moura. Circumspect glances this time, from the dignitaries and the editors of foreign publishing houses. Who was I? If I was Gareth's wife, why wasn't I sitting next to him? Where was Philip? (The front pew looked very empty.) I felt the thoughts and stared at the coffin. There was a damp heat in the church and the smell of cigarette smoke on men's trousers. I wondered if Hugo was hovering over us, smiling at our stooped heads and our crowdedness; whether he was enjoying being both confined to a narrow box and able to roam in the enormous spaces of infinity. Or was that knowing smile reserved for life, for the cynical and dispassionate understanding of humanity?

Of course, Hugo hadn't been Irish at all, not in the sense of parenthood and upbringing. But he could claim a famous Irish revolutionary on the maternal side – and how he preferred that to the East Anglian family Pierce, with the pheasant-shooting acres and ruddy landowners striding through the stubble. There were connections with South Africa too, but how little food for thought that information provided, compared with the glamour of the famous revolutionary. Only Moura would sigh and look away when Hugo began to talk like this. Her own centuries of Blackstone, with no romantic fervour to be found amongst any of them: maybe she felt that was nearer to reality than Hugo's excited word painting of the past.

We stood; we knelt; we sat. The smell of damp and heat was thick in the church; outside by the ruins of the old abbey, under walls that held chipped bas-reliefs still, in a green and cold damp that had endured for centuries, a crowd gathered to watch Hugo being lowered into the ground. A man as different from the small, mediaeval men on the walls as a late twentieth-century human being from a primate. Atheist (but Moura would have warned him that he must expect a burial in the Protestant church, to keep things as they would be expected to be, at Dunane and Blackstone); rational, thoughtful and sceptical in a way those stone men of the past, dancers of the dance of death, could never have known. And I wondered what he would make of it, lying under the foundations of Ireland's oldest abbey – but Hugo wouldn't think anything, of course. He'd have willed himself into non-being as effortlessly as he manipulated time. Nothing

73

numinous, unwelcome could disturb his good-humoured sleep.

I thought of Philip. There must be a reason why he hadn't come, for all the essential elements of his job. Would his careful imitation of Hugo break down when he saw the coffin and he had to come up against the fact of death? The swagger – would that go? Or would he be able to remind himself of his success in the world just in time to avert depression? Had he, like Gareth, spent much less time seeing his father than he would ideally have liked? But there was no Fran to stand in his way – and Moura said he came over to Cliff Hold fairly often. Perhaps it was simply that Philip had known how to be Hugo in life, and wouldn't know how to cope with him dead. Hugo's jokes and aphorisms would last his son a certain length of time and then there would be no one to replenish them. Philip would become like a dusty tape of his father's voice. He would remember one of Hugo's sayings – laughing, holding up his glass of Paddy at Ryan's Bar: 'Someone said that after death there is nothing more that is interesting.'

We knelt for the last time. There was no air in the church, the red velvet of the hassocks came up in a blur and stifled breath. I saw my own white wedding dress in the space where the coffin rested, I saw Philip and myself, bride and groom, on the grain of the cedar-wood lid, smiling and hand-in-hand as if we stood on a cake. Moura's head was lowered in front of me. The bridal couple walked down the aisle and the door opened at the end. A bright sunlight poured in. The organ made a din to wake the dead.

The dignitaries and editors – and the small crowd from Dunane – and Lily, in a green tweed coat and a headscarf pulled down over a face smudged from crying – and Gareth and Moura in the centre – and me: you can see me in the photograph in the *Cork Herald*, to the far side and holding Moura's arm as Hugo goes in. There we all are, some bowed with grief and others wondering if they'll make the plane back to Dublin/Stockholm/Boston if they come up to Cliff Hold afterwards for drinks. In the picture, the sky is so dark that it looks as if something's gone wrong with the inking. No day could naturally be as dark as that. But it was, with the absolute darkness that comes as the other side of Irish fair weather, like the black, blighted side of a potato. Lily's headscarf was the only light thing in the graveyard. In our sombre clothes we stood staring at it, drawn to it: here and there a white sodium flash threw Lily's head into even greater brilliance.

Moura half fell against me when the box went down and the earth was shovelled in. The earth on the coffin was mingled with red roses – and a small handkerchief, Lily's probably, thrown in as pathetic acts of remembrance at the last minute.

And we went back in the car – so slowly that it seemed almost an impossibility to leave the main street at Dunane, to turn up the fuchsia lane, pass the bungalows where people were still sitting and standing, as if something immeasurable in time hadn't just taken place – which was Hugo's physical disappearance into the earth. We sat together: Gareth had spotted a man he knew from an American newspaper and had gone off to find his car with him. I held Moura's hand.

We passed the white houses stacked in steps up the lane. But this time the doors had closed. There were no people standing in the lane. It was as if everything had been quickly shut up and the people had run off. But I didn't say anything. At that depressing speed, we arrived in the end at the top of the hill. Some windows in Cliff Hold came into view. A very faint stripe of pale blue floated over the sea beyond the cliffs and Moura's garden. It hung there a short time, like a thread, between the dark of the morning and the frenetic noise and light of the party later on.

My first thought was, who blew up the balloons? Dazed from the journey in the funeral car, the black suits in church, the grey wash of sky that had dribbled over us all morning, it was a shock to see them: round, like cheerful fat faces pressed together in the hall. Had Gareth pumped his tired lungs into them at his mother's insistence? Had poor Lily been asked to rise early? And who had hung them there while we were burying Hugo in Dunane?

The answer came when Moura, nudging me along the passage, threw open the door of her sitting-room and stood back with an almost vindictive air of achievement. 'There, Minnie,' she said. 'Isn't it lovely?'

In the sitting-room were several waiters in white coats and two parlourmaids in frilly aprons. The head waiter stepped forward. 'Good afternoon, Mrs Pierce.'

Long tables swathed in white damask were packed into the room. Hams and whole sides of salmon; chickens stiff in aspic; bowls of pâté of crab and mackerel and chicken-liver and brandy. Glasses, rows of bottles of spirits and champagne.

'It's just what Hugo would have wanted,' Moura said.

I stood speechless by the long windows, opened now on to the lawn. More tables, equally bridally white, stood on the ledge of grass before the steep path down to Moura's floral staircase. More gold-capped bottles, and goblets, and Moura's silver sauce-boats winking with yellow mayonnaise. Strawberries; meringues like lacy hats. Sugar in more silver bowls.

This must have cost a pretty penny, I heard my mother's voice say in me. And aloud: 'Is it safe to have food out there, Moura? Isn't it going to rain?'

I was right to ask the question with the tone of someone who believes totally in the weather controlling powers of the other. Moura, who had joined me by the window, squeezed my elbow affectionately. 'Not until evening,' she said. She pointed at the narrow band of blue, which had paled and widened, giving a reasonable Southern Irish afternoon, the sort of afternoon the guests at Cliff Hold were well used to being outdoors in, whether scoffing mayonnaise or riding to hounds. 'Perhaps we should go to the front and greet the guests,' Moura said.

I followed her through the room, thinking as I went that this is one way of exorcising Hugo's ghost: there is no room for him now in his favourite armchair by the marble fireplace because his chair has been moved out of the way to make room for the party. There is no room for him at the party, because he is dead. I felt cold suddenly – but only for a moment – walking in Moura's wake to the front door. It was certainly true that Hugo would have loved the idea of a slap-up entertainment. So why did I have to think like this?

The balloons bobbed at us gaily in the breeze from the stout door as we pulled it open. The first cars were sweeping up the lane and turning to park in the field opposite the eagle gates. Moura, beside me and slightly smaller, was braced with energy and anticipation. Two black-suited men reached the gates and walked towards us. She held out her arms in true welcome. And I thought, she is the Spirit of Life, she remembers Hugo in life and celebrates his lifetime. She is right. I am nothing – if anything, the Spirit of Nullity. All the same, I looked away in embarrassment, at the side lawn to Cliff Hold, and the windows of the front room where I slept – as if it might be possible to jump in there like Peter Pan, disappear back into the childhood of unquestioning love of Moura and all her ways.

More people came up the path. I focused my eyes on the orange cats that played under the windowsill of my room. They were so wild they were almost dangerous. As the guests, rearranging their features hastily to smiles in response to Moura's unexpected gaiety, filed past the balloons and off in the direction of the magnificent sitting-room, Moura came up and took my arm.

'Minnie!'

'Yes Moura . . . yes.' I knew what was coming before she spoke.

'Go into the sitting-room and see if – if Gareth has somehow slipped in the back way.' It was painful for her to speak and her voice sounded dry. I knew if Gareth was there it would have meant his leaving his car by Ryan's and going along the beach and up the garden staircase in the rock rather than face the reception line with his mother. It was a form of betrayal that couldn't be measured at the time. But perhaps he'd been 'caught up' leaving the church. Which wasn't much good either. Moura and Hugo, I said to myself, what happened to your perfect family?

'I'll chase away the cats first,' I said. Moura glared at me. She remembers my obstinacy, I thought. 'They'll tear the guests' clothes,' I added, and I took the broom out on the lawn. The cats put up quite a fight: there was a growing army out there by then, and the arriving guests walked nervously round them. In the end they ran round the side of the house and I swept up. Then I went to the sitting-room, as Moura had told me to do.

Gareth was there – as I knew he would be – champagne glass in hand and already swaying on his feet.

The party was noise and glitter, all the faces Hugo loved to watch and laugh at and describe. Waiters in the crowd held out goblets of champagne and plates piled high with salmon and the unending mayonnaise. I caught sight of Gareth a few times, as he stood talking to the garage-and-chain-restaurant-owner from Cork, Johnny Oge – or laughing with one of Hugo's old gang, Johnny Greed or Rex Envy or Lady Sloth (in reality Sally Balmartin). He was flushed and you could see the strain of the whole trip was telling on him badly. As for Moura, she moved among the guests with the grace of a dancer. Her head wasn't stooped any more: she looked up into faces with a look of wonderment and delight, as if she'd never known Hugo had been so much loved and by so many. Her grey eyes were particularly clear that day, I remember. She held her glass of champagne high. I didn't go near mother or son, for fear of provoking the explosion which must come soon.

I went into Hugo's study when I could bear no more of the braying. The old young men from Ryan's Bar had paid their respects and gone, and the Rich American and German castle-owners and the old Ascendancy were in full voice. A few drops of rain had come down on the grass outside the sitting-room windows and the waiters brought in more food and glasses. The crush was intolerable – and the sense of Hugo was very acute. He only made these people amusing by showing up their folly and vanity, after all. Without him they were just what they were, and I couldn't look at it much longer.

Hugo's study was quiet and slightly musty: the party hadn't included it in the manic air of festivity. Apart from a bundle of coats on the bed, there'd be little way of telling it was going on. That was the strength of Cliff Hold: the thick walls that divided room from room and cut off sound at the shutting of a door. I saw Lily go past once – she was in a dress which looked strange to me after so many years of seeing the line of her body only in overalls. She looked preoccupied, and didn't glance in at me. I was glad she didn't: there was something sacrilegious about the way I was sitting in Hugo's swivel leather chair, tipped back and fingers spread on the desk top, as Hugo used to sit when he was thinking and about to write.

The *Cork Examiner* lay open on the desk. Gareth must have been in here, remembering his father in his most characteristic pose. The obituary of Hugo lay on top of the desk. It gave me an eerie feeling, leaning forward in his chair and reading: 'Hugo Pierce, who died on August 27th, was born in 1906 . . . '

I suppose there wasn't much I didn't know. Hugo had joined the staff of *Fortune* magazine in his late twenties, had learnt to be a brilliant journalist and had left in 1936 to found a Trotskyist journal (to which Trotsky himself had contributed), the *New Nation*. By the time he became a novelist in the late forties, he had been a Stalinist fellow-traveller (he broke with the Stalinists over the Moscow Trials), a Trotskyite (he joined the Committee for the Defence of Leon Trotsky), a pacifist and a conservative anarchist. The Cold War had turned him away from political topics and even further in the direction of literature and essays. In the *mai* events in Paris in 1968 he had had a meeting with Jean-Paul Sartre, but had not joined any political affiliation. He had been put forward as a prime contender for the Nobel Prize only last year. His novels and books of criticism include . . .

And so on. It did all seem very long ago. The Russian politics and Hugo's anecdotes of Trotsky and Mexico . . . sitting in the dining-room and pouring port, long after Moura had gone out with secateurs and her long basket to snip away in the garden . . . the red, entranced faces of Gareth and Philip as they heard again of the climb over the wall of Trotsky's villa that Hugo had made with the great man when both were in pursuit of a beautiful and gifted painter . . . The years in Paris . . . the brasserie bars where Hugo met Beckett for what he described as a jar . . . a London quite different from the London I knew, when he'd met and married Moura in the days of youthful communism. Revolutionaries writing poetry . . . and leaving – Hugo amongst them, of course – for the Spanish Civil War: the memories of Hugo's memories brought strong pictures, as if I'd lived through all those years so long ago. And now, he'd made present-day Ireland a magical mixture of history and immediacy too. Through his eyes you saw the Troubles that had always affected the Irish, you saw the famine, and the British troops, and the people's consciousness of the declining way of life here in the West, and their own consciousness of this decline, because, as Hugo said, they were left stranded in the past while as many as could got out and moved on. And what had Hugo made, in the past years, of the violence that had erupted again?

The door had swung shut without my noticing, so when it opened I sat back with a start. The *Cork Examiner* settled back on the desk – I must have been holding it and then let it fall. My ears burnt. I had the absurd feeling that Hugo was coming in, to catch me trespassing on his room. What right did I, the mousy girl 'always dumped here on Moura' as I'd heard him say to a luncheon guest once (affectionately, it was true, but I felt 'dumped' for ever after that) have to question his complicated thoughts on a complicated situation?

It was Gareth – looking in his drunkenness very

feminine, like a parody of Moura when young. His fairish hair stood out in a fluffy halo and his lips were wet. He had the sort of skin that looks as if it's never been shaved.

'Minnie,' Gareth said. 'Good Minnie, eh?'

I should have got up then, but something stopped me. I couldn't move from Hugo's chair. Gareth came unsteadily over to the desk and put his hand on my back just under the shoulders. I could feel the hairs rising on my neck.

'You been reading the obituary?' Gareth said. His years in the States had affected his speech a little and questions ended on an up-note, which in the case of Hugo's death sounded frivolous to English ears. I didn't move.

Gareth swung away and his hand left my back. I felt a surge of relief. He still stood over me, though, the wet lips slightly open.

'They're all saying the Rooneys murdered him – did you know that, Minnie?' he said.

I still didn't move. I wanted to be sick, and then the feeling went away. I felt detached – from myself, from Gareth's voice, from the room lined and thick with Hugo's books. What I'd half-guessed since Moura's call I'd successfully hidden away and would still. I didn't want the present, I'd come here to live again in the past.

'In the woods at Ardo,' Gareth said. I shut my eyes hard and saw red trees leaping. Gareth put his arms on my shoulders again.

'They haven't enough proof,' Gareth said. His legs gave under him suddenly and he sat with a thump on the guests' coats on the end of Hugo's bed.

Even at a time like that I couldn't help thinking, poor Gareth, whatever happened to you, you used to be such a sweet boy. Not a patch on Philip, of course.

Gareth gave an unexpectedly high, jarring laugh. I looked away from him – hoping, I suppose, that if I didn't see him he wouldn't be there.

The laughing started up again. It was hysterical, high-pitched and dry. I had to look at him, and I had to get up and go over and try to comfort him. But he wriggled away from my touch. 'It's – it's so preposterous . . .' he said.

He slumped sideways on the coats. When Lily came in a couple of seconds later to fetch a coat for a guest, she saw Gareth unconscious on the bed, and me standing over him, hands high in horror like a girl in a comic strip. Lily's lips grew thin. She started to loosen Gareth's collar. I left Hugo's room and went down the passage to where the noise of the party was as loud as before – or louder, as it seemed then.

PART TWO

This morning, waiting for the inevitable – for the steps of the Guards, for Moura's face of horror and Lily's cry – I've been marking time: I go through again and again the pages of notes I scribbled down since the day I arrived under leaden skies at Cliff Hold. I see I came here on Friday August 30th: the funeral was Saturday; and I look up now into the first rays of sun since the party on the lawn. Today is Sunday, more than a week has gone by. Marking time, I stare at the bright lettering on the wall calendar in the kitchen: September and it's Sunday 8th. September, month of Moura's orange flowers. They shed petals like painted nails. The cats spitting outside the kitchen window are that violent colour too – or maybe that's just how I see things now. Time and light play odd tricks, when you're marking time.

Better to set out the strange, disjointed sequence of events of the recent past, at least as I saw them. (For soon Lily will come into the kitchen and I'll say, where's Moura? And I'll hear the chopping of dead palmwood in the sub-tropical garden below.) The day will go on.

Sunday, September 1st
Woke up early and lay for a time not knowing what happened last night. Then it came to me. Hugo, so

long above the ways of the world, has been killed. I feel shock, and disbelief: how could anyone want to hurt Hugo?

Then, after the funeral, the party. The woman, Sally (Balmartin?), gin coming down her nostrils at me like a drunken horse. 'You're Minnie, aren't you?' (I remember that, so few people here seem to connect me with the girl of ten years before.) 'Because you ought to . . . you ought . . .'

This woman Sally swayed on her feet. *She* is unchanged, at least: thick red lipstick glued on to the end of a Senior Service and high-heeled court shoes that must have seen her round the dance floors before the war. 'Look after Moura,' she managed to bring out at last. 'She can't . . . understand . . . you know . . . she can't . . .' 'What?' I knew what the answer would be before I spoke. In the cigarette smoke the faces of some of Hugo's old friends and 'characters' lurched and leered. It was dark outside. I must have sat in a trance at Hugo's desk for longer than I thought. 'She can't . . . I mean, who could . . . ?'

The one youngish face present – plump, pasty, the boy from Dunane who'd made good in business locally, who was a councillor in Cork and owned several garages and a chain of butchers' shops – and who was a partner with Ryan of Ryan's Bar and shop too, down in the village – started to walk up to me. Johnny Oge. He'd spent most of the evening with Gareth, but now Gareth was unconscious on his father's bed. No doubt Johnny Oge was under the illusion, like many of the other guests, that I was Gareth's wife, Fran. I backed away.

'Can't face . . . the Rooneys . . .' Sally was saying. 'Well, I'm not surprised she can't face it. Are you?' The voice was thick. A slurp of gin and tonic went down the front of her purple shot-silk dress. The pasty-faced man drew nearer. My legs weakened: in the triangle of my corner I would be trapped for ever with Sally Balmartin and Johnny Oge.

'Hello there, Minnie! You don't mind if I come up and say Hi?' said Johnny Oge. 'Long time no see.'

Sally assumed an expression that was at once distant and daunting. She stayed where she was, though, hanging over her gin and tonic and muttering that she must go off in search of Moura.

'Is it true?' I heard myself saying. 'Are the people in the lane . . . in the white house . . . ?'

Johnny Oge stiffened. He had obviously expected me to show delighted surprise at having been recognized by him at all.

'Moura needs . . . me,' Sally said. But she seemed as unable to move as I was.

'The Rooneys,' I said. 'Is it true?'

It was one way, unconscious and unintentional, of getting out of being stuck in a corner. Johnny Oge turned and walked off, as simple as that. Sally came close and gave me a whack on the back.

'That was a silly girl, Minnie,' she said. 'That was a silly girl.'

And I don't know what happened next, except that Moura must have come up and stood by Sally. Johnny Oge reached the other side of the room, and stood by the marble mantelpiece where Hugo always stood. He glanced over at me in a cold and calculating way so that I felt like a goose, fattened up before winter. But then I am a goose. God give me strength to survive this terrible thing. And to give Moura the help she needs rather than thinking about myself, as I always do.

'Moura darling . . . letsh . . . I mean . . .' Sally waved her falling cigarette at the door. She and Moura would go upstairs and lie on Moura's bed. There, perhaps, Moura would have a chance to cry at last. I wanted to go to the kitchen. I wanted Lily. But on the way out of the room a knot of old party hands held me up.

'Flann O'Brien, excuse me, did not write that.'

. 'I beg your bloody pardon. It was the year we went to Egypt together. Up the Nile.'

'He never went to Egypt, damn your puking little soul.'

Oh, how I remember that drunken talk: how Hugo used to love it, it seemed he could never get enough.

'Yes, up the Nile the two of us. *At Swim-Two-Birds.*'

'Ach, fer cryin' out loud.'

Even the most recent visitors and acquirers of property in the country feel free to assume a 'brogue'. I lowered my head, like Moura stooping at the entrance to the Protestant cemetery. But a hand gripped me as I pushed my way to the door.

'We'd better talk,' said Johnny Oge. And he pulled me along the pebble corridor to the dining-room, empty now except for dirty plates and a smell of stale cigarettes and food.

Johnny Oge was one of the few 'characters' whose company was enjoyed by Hugo and who yet did not figure in one of his books. This may have been to do with his lowly origins, manic energy and determination to succeed – maybe he was an example of how to manipulate capitalism, in Hugo and Philip's eyes, and thus a sort of working-class hero. I'd always been uneasy when he arrived at Cliff Hold and sat in Moura's sitting-room with a glass of Jamieson's held in fingers that looked as if they'd never fully formed. Moura didn't like him either. We didn't discuss him, but he left behind a pall which hung over the house for hours after he'd gone. Now, I wondered why he singled me out to tell me the last chapter of Hugo's story – when he'd hardly seen me in the old days at Cliff Hold. Or perhaps it's so obvious, I thought at first, that I hardly need to wonder: as Moura's confidante I can be useful to him in some way. But when he spoke, I saw it was my unthinking talk that had hit home.

First, Johnny Oge asked me if I knew the Rooneys. When I said no, I couldn't say I remembered them, or even the mention of the name, in my day here, he said: 'Well, that's the thing, Minnie. It's all been in the last four or five years. And a great problem for everyone it's been.'

The story came out that Hugo had, in the past couple of years at least, become less and less popular in the area. This had been due to a friendship with a young woman who had settled in one of the white houses in the lane: she'd come after her parents-in-law had moved there, and she'd come with a young baby and a husband who visited her from time to time. She was Kitty Rooney.

Johnny Oge's plump fingers waved as he talked. There was nothing wrong, of course, with Hugo making such a friendship – think of Parnell and Kitty O'Shea, he said, and laughed, and I remembered Moura telling me how her mother's mother, in that long line of Blackstone matriarchs, had 'despised Kitty O'Shea'. Anyway, Johnny Oge said, it was no more than a friendship: Hugo was an old man. People knew he was a kind man. He took up Kitty Rooney as a cause. And wherever he turned, he came up against a stone wall.

Kitty Rooney's husband Des was the trouble. He and Kitty had lived in a flat in Cork, where the baby was born. Soon after the birth Des started staying out all night; and after that there were visits from men who left things in a front room that was kept locked. Kitty had had to live in the kitchen and the bedroom, with the baby. She didn't suspect that guns or anything like that were being dumped there. And she was right, in that respect: finding the key in Des's pocket one day and going in, she'd seen cash registers, TVs, that kind of thing. When she remonstrated with her husband, he beat her violently. That was the start of it all.

Hugo's face kept coming to me, as Johnny Oge talked. I saw it hover above Kitty Rooney – the dark, pretty girl in the lane must have been Kitty Rooney – as she fled her husband after continued violence from him and moved to her parents-in-law in the white shoe-box house in the lane. I saw Hugo's concern, when he heard her story in Ryan's one morning, downing his Guinness in the first cloud of tobacco smoke of the day. I saw the first meeting, when he passed Kitty Rooney on her way up from the shops in Dunane and she asked him, suddenly, desperately, for help. Because, Johnny Oge said, Des was coming out from Cork to the village when he felt in the mood. Sometimes he sent men in fast cars who pinned Kitty and her baby against the hedge and threatened to kidnap the baby if she didn't come back at once to the flat in Cork. She was his wife, she had deserted him and the child was legally his – and so on. (I saw Hugo's concern; and his vanity. For all the scoffing at Yeats, and there were plenty of jokes to be had there – Hugo taught Philip too to laugh at Yeats while half respecting his poetic genius – for all the determined attempt not to be a vain old man, Hugo had been fast on the way to becoming one when I'd last been at Cliff Hold. He wore shabby clothes. He ambled in an exaggerated way, as if to show he had no care to make women look at him any more. But they did: apart from his famous name, he had the nearest thing to a magnetic personality most people had ever known. His very insouciance betrayed his vanity.) Now I saw him wondering, when she was so unlike the other women he met with Moura or the women he met at the parties he went to on his rare visits to New York or Rome or Berlin to visit publishers, or collect a prize, if Kitty Rooney would just see him as a pathetic old man. It was an irresistible challenge – although this wasn't what Johnny Oge was saying as I sat there and saw it all.

Hugo had taken up Kitty Rooney's fight against Des. Divorce was out of the question. Legal separation was not, however: the best lawyer from Dublin was hired by Hugo; the evidence of Des's domestic brutality was overwhelming. (He was too clever to get caught with stolen goods, though, and he emerged as an innocent young man with his foot on the first rung as an insurance salesman.) Despite the evidence of cruelty – and this was where Hugo had 'gone over the top', as Johnny Oge expressed it, Des Rooney was awarded custody of the child. And one day – it must have been about six months ago – a car had arrived with one of his colleagues, as Des called them, at the wheel. The baby was handed over by Des's parents while Kitty Rooney screamed for everyone to hear in the lane as far down as Ryan's. It later emerged her father-in-law had locked her in her room. She was told she could take the child for one weekend in four, collecting him from the flat in Cork. Hugo hired a private detective and put him on Des, in the hope of a prison sentence for violence and theft.

Johnny Oge got up and went over to the sideboard, where half-empty bottles of whiskey stood in a litter of screwed-up napkins and cigarette butts. He poured a good quadruple Jamieson's into a used glass. Then he came back and sat down and drew his chair up even closer to me. I leaned back. I felt sick. I could just see a knot of people in the corridor outside.

'You ask yourself why I'm telling you all this,' Johnny Oge said. 'Well, I'll tell you, Minnie.'

In the dark of the lawn beyond the window a small light moved. I remembered, suddenly, how Lily had used to lock the cats up at night, in the old coop by the steps at the top of the staircase garden. She'd had a pencil torch (Gareth had given it her one Christmas) but the cats are uncontrollable now and Lily's too old.

'I'm telling you Des Rooney is no angel,' Johnny Oge said in a soft voice made glutinous by the whiskey as it went down. 'He's wild and wicked – I'll grant you that.'

The knot of people in the corridor drifted into the room. There was a girl with red hair in a fringe and lips stained berry-red with wine. She was pursued by an Irish peer in a tweed suit as old and trampled-looking as a field – and an American, Ken Gluttony himself, who, true to form, held half a chicken in his wide hands. I suffered a pang for Hugo: he'd have loved that sight, and the way Ken Gluttony tried to woo the girl while at the same time refusing to keep the food more than one inch away from his mouth. The girl backed away and almost stumbled against my chair. Johnny Oge brought his whiskey breath right up to my face and lowered his voice to a whisper: 'Des shouldn't have lifted a hand to poor Kitty. But there's always two sides to these things, Minnie. She poked into his business. Now you may have Women's Lib ideas, but no man likes a woman who pries into his secrets.'

Bluebeard, I thought. I tried to rise – I could stand no more of Johnny Oge – but the red-haired girl was now leaning heavily against the back of my chair. She, too, was trying to get away. The Irish peer was offering a visit to his eighteenth-century castle in

County Clare. I recognized him, by his slow drawl, as Lord Sloth of Hugo's very funny take-off of Somerville and Ross, in his novel *Three Day Event*.

'But what I'm saying is,' Johnny Oge went on relentlessly, 'what I'm saying, Minnie, is the rumours are just scandalous. Just out of this world!'

'Rumours,' I said. I knew as soon as I spoke that the group of people near me – Lord Sloth and Ken Gluttony and the girl with the red-wine lips, all thought I'd said Rooneys. I just knew it, seconds before they took the word and tossed it up in the air.

'Rooneys,' said Ken Gluttony, holding the half-gnawed chicken to one side. 'I hear there's foul play suspected . . . you know . . . with old Hugo.'

'Excuse me,' Johnny Oge said. He stood up. No one paid any attention to him. I saw that in the eyes of these people Johnny Oge simply doesn't exist.

'I like Hugo,' Lord Sloth said. He paused, he wondered whether to correct the tense, as people do when speaking of someone just dead. (There was no more suitable moment, I thought, than then for Hugo to reappear. His characters discussing his possible murder. He would relish that.)

'I liked Hugo,' Lord Sloth corrected himself at last. 'But, in a way, he had it coming to him, you know.'

He stared down the cleavage of the red-haired girl as he spoke. What he meant was, Hugo shouldn't have messed about in the affairs of people like the Rooneys.

Ken Gluttony held up the half-skeleton of the chicken. The bones glistened in his fingers. He hunted for a napkin, found a soiled one, wrapped them up and threw them down on the table in front of Johnny Oge.

'I guess it's none of our business,' he said. 'Hey, we oughta be getting back.'

Johnny Oge pushed his way into the middle of the group. They stared at him – there was a look of dim

95

recognition on the part of Lord Sloth – then they decided he'd had too much to drink and was of no interest anyway. The party was over, until someone as amusing as Hugo appeared on the horizon and started something going again. But that day would be a long time coming.

'Des Rooney was certainly in Dunane on the morning of Hugo's death,' Johnny Oge said in his loud, thick voice. 'Kitty'd gone into Cork the night before and snatched the baby back and you may say she had every right, being the mother. You may say that.'

Leaving the dining-room meant pushing past Johnny Oge now. This Ken Gluttony proceeded to do. He even went so far as to lay his hefty hands on Oge's sleeve – leaving, I saw, a thumb-shaped mark of chicken grease. Behind the group, out in the corridor, I saw Lily go past. She was carrying a bowl of broth. Reviving her beloved Gareth, probably; Gareth, who'd got drunk, no doubt, because his mother had told him even before the funeral that his father hadn't died a natural death. Now I saw why Gareth wouldn't face the reception line at the front door with Moura. He was in a state of shock. And ever since the beginning of the party he'd been having to listen to Johnny Oge – as we were all having to listen to him now.

'Des wanted the baby back,' Johnny Oge said. 'But for all the aggravation in the world, Des would never kill a man. Not Des.'

Lord Sloth knew how to deal with a man like Johnny Oge. He half turned to him, said, 'How simply fascinating,' and half accidentally trod on Oge's toe so as to get to the door. That's how they train them to deal with similar situations at public school, I suppose.

'Shall we see if the Poissonnerie is open?' the red-haired girl said to Lord Sloth.

'I could do with some seafood,' said Ken Gluttony.

'I don't feel like driving all the way to Cork,' Lord Sloth said. 'Let's just go to your place for a nightcap.'

The American, whose 'place' was hung with Murillos and Titians and Ruysdaels and had over fifty rooms, nodded in agreement. And they left. They walked out into the corridor as if they'd never seen Johnny Oge in their lives. I heard the red-haired girl saying in a vague way that they must find Moura. But they didn't bother – when their voices had gone down into the hall and out through the front door, there was silence. Johnny Oge stood staring after them for a while. Then he went out too and I was left alone.

I went to bed, but I didn't sleep. How Moura's world has changed, since the days when we all went on picnics to the cove under Ardo – since the walks on the cliff and the jokes that Hugo would never come too. He must have taken to walking alone, then: down the lane with the white houses, past the house where Kitty Rooney wept at the injustice of her life. Poor Hugo! He would do anything to protect the victims of injustice. He can't have thought he'd die though . . . and I saw the lunging figure of Des Rooney . . . and I shivered in the bed that smelt like a pond from a year-long lack of use. As I lay awake I could feel them cold all round me: Moura, with her cool good taste, her frozen refusal to face the facts; the sons Philip and Gareth, glacial in their mountain-climb to the tops of their careers; Hugo, detached, keeping his observations on humanity at an amusingly low temperature. Des Rooney and his brother . . . as I fell asleep I saw them hot . . . a blot of dark red . . . an accident, an act of violence so hot it blots the memory. I woke hot, as if this unwanted heat had crept up the fuchsia lane and into the cold house.

Monday, September 2nd

In my room is a tapestry that must have come over with Moura from Blackstone, when she came to live here. It is tall and dark and green, and in a forest where there are people riding on horses with long, thin legs, there are also a dying fox, gored by hounds, a rabbit in a cross-stitching of snowdrops and winter aconites, and a young woman gathering sticks. On the horses are a distinguished, elderly man, a father, a seigneur – a woman in a white coif that looks as it sails out on her head like a white bird; and several young men in green jerkins and red pointed hats. They are going towards the edge of the wood: the light in thinning trees shows that. Only the girl gathering sticks will be left behind in the forest. Her hair is black, the wools of her face are ruddy. None of the hunting party, on their steeds with absurdly narrow and elongated haunches, turns to look back at her.

We went out riding in the afternoon yesterday. If our party didn't look quite like the group in the tapestry, there was the same light and air, the same dapple of green and orange in the woods at Ardo. That was where Moura insisted on going. And I – dazed from the party the night before, the half-haunted sleep in the room at the end of the passage no doubt originally intended for me (for when I wandered back into Hugo's room Gareth was still unconscious on his father's bed) – I had agreed to the plan before I knew what it would entail. There were four of us: Moura and Gareth, and the woman Sally who had come over 'to help with the clearing up' and me. It must be ten years since I was on a horse. We mounted just outside the gates to Cliff Hold and climbed slowly into a world of sky, a wide yellow sweep of light and cloud that folded in the swells in the green land as if they were part of the clouds.

I didn't want to go over to Blackstone or to ride up the side of the hill to Ardo. I felt as if I were being sewn into a drama I had never suspected – into a moving tapestry. Even the shadow of the young woman gathering sticks was there, up in the woods where Hugo had fallen. I smelt the pain of the dying fox; the orange of the beech leaves underfoot was part of the livid colour of the violence that seemed to be all around. Twigs in the trees were round and knotted fists, pigeons' nests, cannonballs of twig and moss. Moura's white headscarf fluttered ahead of us like a white dove.

What am I to say about the reactions of these people to the probable murder of their adored Hugo? How can I tell, in the face of Moura's perfect breeding, her refusal to allow that anything in life's plan could have 'gone wrong', how much she suffers from the rumours, the open knowledge of Hugo's champion-ing of the young woman whose ruddy-faced shadow flits between the trees at Ardo – a sense of duty so strong that this most olympian of men was drawn into a small-town web, a sink of corruption and domestic brutality that brought him to a violent end? How can she bear it? Why does she insist on going back to the place treacherous with banks of leaves over deep holes, where he ostensibly tripped and fell? There's nothing to see there. The Gardai swept up most of the leaves in looking for clues. There weren't any, of course. The area looks bald, shaved round the exposed roots of the trees.

Of the two allusions to Hugo's death that I've heard since Johnny Oge's revelations at the party, Sally's was the more confusing and Lily's was the first time I've heard menace in her voice.

I asked Sally, as we rode through the woods at Ardo, what she thought had really happened, what

Johnny Oge meant by his protestations of the Rooneys' innocence, whether the Gardai did suspect them but could find no proof. 'Quite honestly,' Sally said, 'none of that is the point.' Her wide-barrelled, ginny face stared back at me over a hunting-stock of a vivid pink. I could see her in Kenya, in Malaya, on the velds and verandas where Hugo had placed her as the eternal memsahib. She waved in the direction of Moura, a small figure on her bay mare in the belt of trees where they space out into field. 'The point is not to let *her* think about it too much. Bad for her, y'know.'

'But if. . .' I felt in as much of an impasse with Sally as I had with Johnny Oge. 'Did they – and who *are* they exactly?'

'That's the thing.' Sally broke into a trot: I followed – frightened already at the unaccustomed movement, waiting to fall as I knew I would. 'No, one doesn't want to be too mixed up in these things,' Sally said. 'There's the brother of Des Rooney, you see. One simply doesn't want to be mixed up in it.'

The mare fell back into a walk again. All the same, we were reaching the edge of the woods and Gareth was close, his fair hair stuck down under his cap. He looked as if he'd suffered from the night before. As if he could hardly believe his mother's insistence in going to the place of Hugo's death so soon after the burial. He tried to smile at us, but his face was frozen. Sally came close to me so that my horse, aware already of my lack of confidence, shifted irritably. 'No one can prove anything,' Sally said in a fast, gruff whisper. 'It's better left alone.'

What am I to think? I lie in bed and stare at the tapestry, at men and women in a French forest – dead for centuries now and in the first place dead, because modelled on figures from mythology: Diana the Huntress, Demeter on the winter-flower-studded floor of the forest, gathering white flowers for her daughter's return. They are far away from me – but no further than the white house in the lane, Hugo's fall and Des Rooney's lurching run. I try to think of Philip, to believe he'll come soon and – and what? Put an end to the unease here, the rumours and the whispers and Moura's strange look? But Lily comes in instead, with a cup of tea.

'Lily,' I said as I took the cup and moved my eyes from the tapestry to her familiar face, 'What's going to happen here? What happened exactly? You told me Hugo'd been very ill.'

'He was ill,' Lily said. 'He wasn't right in his mind, Minnie.'

'You mean he shouldn't have – fought for Kitty Rooney . . . ?' I remembered Johnny Oge's crude joke about Parnell and Kitty O'Shea.

Lily sat down on the end of my bed. Behind her was the wall with the tapestry, the window where the orange cats played, and the great blue and white vase plundered by Moura's ancestors at the sack of the Summer Palace at Peking. Lily looks frail and grim today: the effort of the funeral and then the party – and not having gone home in several nights – has taken its toll. In the silence after my last, awkward question, I thought how I could best soothe Lily – whether she would want to hear about my mother, whom she had never liked, or would want to be asked about her brother Old Tom at Blackstone. In the end I asked about Old Tom. Because we were there yesterday, after the ride in the woods at Ardo: Moura had insisted on going out the far side of the woods, on to the hill above the house.

'He's no better, Minnie,' Lily said, relieved at not

having to think about Hugo. 'Doesn't know what he says. Now he's always after laying down the can opener and he can't for the life of him think where it's gone.'

'But why stay on here any longer?' I said. 'I mean, Gareth's here. And I'm here,' I added without much force. 'If he needs you, Lily . . .'

'I need to stay here,' Lily muttered. She got up and went over to the window. The orange cat, on seeing her there, gave out a mad hissing. 'Something's got to be done about it,' Lily said. 'Something has to be done, that's for sure.'

When we were out of the woods at Ardo we stopped and looked around in all directions: the flat top of the hill above Blackstone makes you do that. It's a landscape as remote as the tapestry in my room – but remote in a different way, like a Chinese screen, unfolding a wash and fine pictography of mountains, blue of sea and river, orange reeds sticking up like cranes' legs in the marsh. There's none of the closeness, the distant, two-dimensional intimacy of the wood, the moving haunches of the horses, the backs of people so near they can be seen to be complete strangers. Instead, there's the sense of everything being impossibly far away. The house at Blackstone could have been painted in at a later date, by an artist who had paid a brief visit to the West. The village is a pen-and-ink scrawl. Behind the house is the kitchen garden; and this is where we came down first, with Moura thinking aloud, as she always does when she is excited about something.

'We can ride through the hole in the wall. Shall we Gareth?'

'If you like.' Gareth was frowning, he didn't want

this expedition. Nor did Sally, who kept glancing at me and shaking her head.

'They won't keep up the repairs,' Moura said. Her voice was shrill. 'It's Cousin Ottoline. She can't bring herself to think of these things.'

There's a gap in the brick wall, a larger gap than the one I remember the last time I was here. Nettles grow in the fallen brick. My horse slithered as we went over and I nearly fell, again. But the kitchen garden took me in as it had when I was a child, here with Philip on our bikes, escaping for the day from Cliff Hold. I lagged behind, as Moura, with Gareth and Sally in tow, trotted through the neglected orchard, under the walls where the shadows of trained apricots are still etched out.

Moura called up at the back of the house in that childlike, high-pitched voice. The house, shut off by the southern wall of the kitchen garden and flanked by ancient yews, seemed totally deaf.

It's true Cousin Henry and Cousin Ottoline have let the vegetables go, and the fruit and the beds of stocks and Sweet Williams and sweet peas; and the herbs, the banks of sage and parsley and lovage have spread over the paths. There are occasional feathery signs of carrot, or the head of a cabbage, or potato – but the ground is covered in chickweed. The greenhouse has a smashed roof and the fig inside has small, green fruit. Yet the kitchen garden has still the same bitter, strong, hot smell, as if all the summers in this low-lying spot by the fields that were never reclaimed from swamp, had accumulated to a tropic: a still, stagnant abundance of earth and leaf. It is a place for children. Slugs lie for hours on the narrow paths bordered by lavender. Birds nest under the eaves of Old Tom's cottage, a building that is as strange as a house in a fairytale, for it is half built in the wall of the kitchen garden and the other half sticks out of the back into the small village of Blackstone. The roof of Old Tom's cottage has even more missing slates than it had ten years ago. I stopped by it, feeling foolish on my horse, hearing the echo of Moura's voice in the front of the house by now, on sunken lawns under the yews.

A child – I thought it was a boy at first – wandered down the path towards me. I had the feeling I knew the child, that I saw myself – or Philip – walking up to me past the nailed arms of the fruit trees on the wall.

The child nodded and walked past. She was about ten years old, in dungarees. She knocked on Old Tom's door and he came out.

Lily moves by the window. Two orange kittens have jumped up on the sill. In their fight, hair stands on end, ears, tattered and half bitten off, lie flat against the head.

'Lily,' I beg her as she comes to take the cup of tea and carry it away untasted without a word, 'Lily, why did Old Tom do that? And the child – it was the same child, wasn't it?'

'Do what?' Lily puts the cup down on the chest of drawers and moves back to the window. The cats are a pretext for staying: she pulls the window up with a jerk and swings out at them. Still locked in fight, they tumble off the ledge.

'You know, Lily.' Sitting up in bed, I can see Lily's head move back into line with the tapestry again, into the patch of pale wall beyond the trees where Blackstone lies.

I didn't know what to say to Old Tom. He was so old. His face was like a screwed-up leaf. His cap had been so long on his head that it would have been impossible to take it off without his hair, grey-green with dirt and age, coming away too. How does he manage here without Lily? And why should he remember me anyway? When I was last here I was the age of the child who is standing patiently by his door, waiting for me to go away. 'Old Tom,' I said all the same, 'I'm Minnie. A friend of Philip's. Do you remember me?'

Old Tom looked bewildered from me to the child. I dismounted and went up to him. The child went and stood by the horse. I heard myself speak in the loud voice people reserve for the young, foreign or mad. 'And Hugo. A friend of Hugo,' I bellowed. 'At Cliff Hold.'

Old Tom stared. He shuffled off along the path, turning to beckon me to follow. His back was so humped it was round, like a sack propelling itself along when he walked. I had a disloyal thought about Moura: couldn't she look after Old Tom better than this? His ill-health; his poverty; his wandering mind. But to think this was to forget I'd returned to a strange country that seems stranger still today. I'd accepted things more readily then. Old Tom was Yeatsian – but to be found everywhere in the rural West even now.

Old Tom stopped at the edge of what had once been the vegetable allotment. I followed him.

'What is it Tom?'

I thought, shall I tell him Lily is at Cliff Hold and will be home soon? That even now she's very likely on her way over . . . But I knew somehow that Lily wasn't on her way. A small dog ran out of the cottage and the horse shied. But the child caught hold of the bridle and I followed Old Tom further along the path and then right into the cabbage bed, with its rotten leaves and stalks half broken off above ground.

It seems strange that when I tell Lily this morning of Old Tom in the cabbage patch at Blackstone, she simply nods: a confirming nod, as if I hadn't just recounted another piece of madness of Old Tom's. 'But why, Lily?' I say. And she half smiles even, replying: 'Well, maybe that's how it was.'

Old Tom's little dog – a mongrel with a snappy face – started to gallop towards the gap in the wall we'd all come through – it was as if it always did this when Old Tom went in amongst the cabbages. The dog set up a howling and barking that would have brought anyone less sleepy than Cousin Ottoline and Cousin Henry out of the house. And Old Tom, as I stood there watching, stooped down and picked up a large cabbage leaf and put it in his mouth. Those Dutch pictures of vegetable heads – Moura used to show them to me in a book – Old Tom looked now as if he consisted entirely of cabbage. And yet it wasn't a joke, although Old Tom laughed and cried at the same time, dribbling on the leaf that hid his face. He stretched out his arms. The dog barked more wildly. Slow as a scarecrow, the figure of Old Tom now swung to the west, to the gap in the wall, to the woods at Ardo beyond. His right arm pointed there, his left arm dropped.

'Is he trying to . . . to . . . show what someone did?' I say stupidly to Lily. My first thoughts at the time had been of mime – then of mask – 'Did he see someone cover his face?'

'Maybe it's what he saw,' Lily says. And this time she goes out of the room. It's getting late for doing potatoes for lunch. So I lie still in the same position, staring at the tapestry. And I see the trees thin out, and the ride down the hill to Blackstone, and a man running out towards me – only I can't see who it is because his face is covered by a cabbage leaf. Then the long, dark rooms at Blackstone – the dark, after the white outside; the panelling in tiny squares of old oak; the smell of dirty water, as if the house, like a derelict Venetian palace, stood right in the river and the stagnant tide oozes up into the rooms.

Cousin Henry and Cousin Ottoline were on a sofa with a high, red velvet back, in the second room – Blackstone is too old to have corridors – the room with the charred-looking painting of Moura's sixteenth-century ancestors over a stone fireplace inscribed with carvings of men praying, hewing, milling. All you can see of the ancestors is a girl in a white dress with a stiff, white, plain face. Cousin Henry and Cousin Ottoline look as ghostly. They must have been woken by Moura from one of their sleeps, which carry them through afternoons heavy with the smell of wet meadow coming in the window, to digestive biscuits and tea.

For all the pretence of paying a visit to make sure these remote cousins and dependants keep the place in order, Moura was really, I think, showing Blackstone to Gareth again. Reminding him of it. She glanced at him often, as she might a lover – yet she didn't, oddly, give the impression that she found him lovable. She was too bound up in herself for that. She was demanding something of him; and the more she demanded, the more rigid and inhuman her son's expression became.

'Ah Minnie,' Moura said. Obediently I went up and greeted the cousins – they held out hands as white and dry as wafers. 'I was saying,' Moura said, 'that Gareth pretends to remember his grandmother hardly at all.' Moura was standing, declaiming. I know her in this mood and my heart sank. 'But Minnie certainly remembers her – *she* hasn't forgotten because she went to live in New York. Minnie, tell Gareth what his grandmother was like, dear.'

It's an impossible question, of course, and it isn't meant to be answered. I didn't dare look over at Gareth, to see how he was taking the attack. Appealing to Cousin Henry and Cousin Ottoline wasn't any help either: they might as well have been painted on the high, velvet cushions. I looked instead at the window, with its small panes and ancient, distorted glass. Not for the first time at Blackstone, I wanted to get out.

'Your grandmother was a very remarkable woman,' Moura said. 'I'm amazed you remember so little about her.'

Gareth sulked like a ten-year-old. A bee from the swampy garden where over-blown peonies tangle with long grass and buttercups of a liquid yellow, banged itself against the small panes. The buzzing went on uninterrupted. From the shadows of the yews outside it was getting late. We had to get the horses back.

'She often asked for you when she was dying,' Moura said.

The room sighed with guilt, with the dark hours of *ennui* and suffering that had sunk into the walls and came out in scenes like this: a palimpsest of human pain, reconciliations, compromise. Blackstone has always made me uncomfortable. I wanted to get back to the sea, to the garden that falls down on to rocks as if it had been hurled there and caught in mid-fall by a camera. I coughed. I made my way to the door, oak-thick as a door in a mediaeval prison.

'We should be going,' Gareth said.

'But darling,' Moura broke in, as movements were made and the first faint smiles appeared on the faces of Cousin Henry and Cousin Ottoline, 'you *will* go and lock up the Gun Room and put the key back where it belongs.' She paused; Gareth and I must both have seen the peg in the back larder where the Gun Room keys hang – must both have heard: '*Not* to be taken; guns are dangerous; do you hear?' from the years Gareth thinks he has forgotten and I have for so long tried to forget. 'Minnie'll do it,' Moura said quickly, as Gareth stood unmoving. 'Hurry up, darling.' And she thrust the keys at me. I was glad to be out.

The Gun Room, over the stables and on the opposite side of the house to the kitchen garden, was reached by climbing spiral stairs of stone that smelt always 'washed down' as if living horses and dogs inhabited the place. But – as I knew too well from the fears of the past – there were only dead, embalmed or stuffed animals in the dark room at the top of the stairs. An aviary of birds, caught in a frozen hop on a branch. Pale adders in jars, pickled in alcohol. A stuffed boar's head, with yellow tusks that looked as if they'd come down over your hand. And the famous stuffed salmon: Gareth had caught it in the Blackwater when he was still very young; Philip had looked bored. So Moura had been showing Gareth his fish again! I had to look in – to see it in the dim light, in a glass coffin with a few pebbles under the belly, to simulate river conditions. I had to knock my hand against the boar's head – and to look up at the guns on the wall. And I had to see Old Tom and the child, standing as quiet as masterpieces of the taxidermist's art. Did they really think I might not see them? 'I've come to lock up,' I said.

Old Tom smiled and shuffled as he had in the cabbage patch – and the child looked straight at me as if she was as pure and deaf and mute as Old Tom – and I let them down the spiral stairs and locked up. They went ahead of me, across the stable yard and out in front of the house. Old Tom was bent so low he might have been searching the lawn for weed, or unsightly stones. The child ran without looking right or left. At the window – as Old Tom went by as hunched in himself as a tortoise – stood Moura. She was at the window, looking out. Her gaze went over Old Tom's back, to the swamp of overgrown garden beyond the yews.

In the end everyone was out on the lawn – and Moura went off in search of the horses and Sally. Cousin Henry and Cousin Ottoline stood at the door – too pale and tired even to show relief. And I could have sworn I saw a woman behind them – taller than either of them, sweet-faced but grim, staring out.

Moura's mother: she made each trick of the light recreate her in the old house. The stairs – shallow steps and dark wood banisters – twisted in the shaft of light that was for a moment her long white dress or the bend of her neck. The pictures – of hills and deer and butterflies and birds – showed in tarnished glass the reflection of her face and her dark coil of hair. I remember her, it's true, when Moura took me over to Blackstone as a child. I remember too the stories of her famous 'eye', which locals said had the power to do anything. I saw it in Moura yesterday afternoon – but it was one of my states coming on, of course – the aura, the whiteness, the fear and the blur. Her eye, as Hugo's had seemed to do in the marble motif on the fireplace at Cliff Hold, stared straight out at me as strong and blue as a Greek bead.

(Moura, with strangers, had pretended to laugh about her mother's supposed powers. 'You need to keep on the right side of her,' she'd say to visiting journalists who came to see Hugo and were then taken to see Blackstone afterwards (it was as if Hugo felt he couldn't be explained unless his wife's background was actually seen). 'She's got "the eye", you know.'

No, they didn't know. Even when young I saw their baffled expressions: was this woman, an artist in her own right and the wife of the ultra-rational 'great author' Hugo Pierce, trying to tell them of the super-natural? They laughed uneasily – I always knew the laughter was uneasy when it was loud and over-long. 'What does she do with the eye?' they said. 'Oh, she only uses it when there's been some disloyalty to the family,' Moura said . . . 'Her enemies, you know.')

The green of the waterlogged meadows soothed my head on the ride home. I hardly saw the little band of men at the gate to Blackstone – though I wonder now why Moura talked to them so long and in so low a voice. I concentrated instead on Sally's prosaic figure, her way of sitting astride her horse as if she'd been born in that position. Sally was certainly not the possessor of an 'eye'.

I kept behind Sally as we took the long way home – and it's only this morning that I see we went that way for a purpose. We rode down the valley and over the bridge and up again before we came into Dunane. So we went to Cliff Hold past the white houses. Moura rode alongside Gareth as they passed the Rooneys' house. But he looked ahead and said nothing.

In the tapestry, beyond the trees where the wool is thin and the light is coming in, there is now a figure pacing back and forth. The men on their long-legged horses are still riding in the forest and the dying fox is still being gored by the hounds. But the woman, the wife and mother who had been riding with the seigneur, has dismounted and her horse has disappeared. She's walking beyond the trees, on the hills that lead down to Blackstone. And her eyes are looking out of the tapestry straight into the room.

Lily comes back in; she is irritated now. 'You'd

better be thinking of getting up,' she says. 'Do you not feel yourself again today, Minnie?'

I will get up, I tell her. But I dread the day. Gareth will be hiding somewhere in the house or down on the rocks where the staircase garden ends; Moura will be stalking him – yes, she wants in some way to rope him in. And I'll be caught between the two – drawn into a tapestry where, when the hunt has run its course, a man must fall in the leaves and die.

'And Mrs Pierce says will you help with the lunch,' Lily says. 'Mrs Gareth's due to arrive this morning. Mrs Pierce has gone in to Ryan's for pork.'

My next time alone with Moura, which was brief – in the garden and interrupted by Sally, who said she was going home to change out of her riding clothes and would be back later for dinner – didn't give much indication of what was going on in Moura's mind.

She was cutting at the yellowing palm fronds in the tropical garden. I was to catch them and put them on the rubbish pile. But I was soon up to my knees in jagged palm leaves.

'Moura,' I said, 'd'you think one can not . . . I mean . . . mind things. I mean . .'

'My mother paid no attention to things of that sort,' Moura's answer came back quickly. 'They were simply below her and that was that.'

A heavy branch came down, almost crowning me with palm. Moura, on the rickety garden chair, leaned forward and disappeared into the tree. 'There've been rats here,' was her next remark. 'We'll have to put down some poison, Minnie.'

'But – you don't really think the Rooneys – ' I had to shout into the tree.

Moura's face appeared again. Her hair was dishevelled. I felt suddenly that there was something grotesque and frightening about her and the world she had spun around herself. She climbed down and stood close to me in the leaves – as always I could smell the faintly perfumed lozenges she sucked for her dry throat. She pointed derisively down at the leaves. 'You hardly picked any of this up,' Moura said. She gave a little laugh and threw back her head. 'You saw those men at the gates of Blackstone, did you, Minnie?'

'Yes.' I couldn't think what the men had to do with it. But Moura often jumped about like this – it was up to the other person to piece together the puzzle at the end.

'Such a pity Cousin Ottoline doesn't give them anything to do,' Moura said. She sighed; in her sigh I saw the long childhood at Blackstone, the childhood that had never really come to an end when she married Hugo and moved to another family house by the sea. (Not that Moura was rich – but it would be out of the question for either Cliff Hold or Blackstone to be sold. Moura had a small income and that was all – it was Hugo who knew what it had been like to be poor, despite his well-off family in Essex, for they'd cut him off when he joined the Communist Party – it was Hugo who'd made money from his books, given too much away, lost a good half of it in the early days on a left-wing paper in Mexico which he'd co-edited with a famous Mexican poet and revolutionary – Hugo who'd taught the boys the philosophy of taking what you can from 'the capitalists', even if 'the capitalist' was a rich girl who thought she was liked for her-self.)

'They want to help us, Minnie.'

'What do you mean?' I was jolted from Philip, in my mind's eye in a smart restaurant in New York, to a picture of the drive at Blackstone, the small lodge with a roof like a pointed hat, and the three old men, so old they must have known Moura as a child, standing by her on her horse.

'You'll see.' Moura's dramatic side was coming to the fore. She pushed past the thin trunks of young palm shoots on the way out to the steps up to the house. She turned once. 'Did you see Old Tom there, by the way?'

'Yes, I did.' I hurried after Moura, feeling as always that I'd missed a unique opportunity to plumb the secrets of her temperament, the unknown pattern of her life. But then, Moura always made me feel like that. 'Old Tom had a cabbage leaf in his mouth,' I said breathlessly as we climbed. Moura's faded cotton skirt, torn and showing old cotton knickers, climbed above me. It stopped. Moura looked down.

'Did he, Minnie?' She gave an indulgent chuckle. 'Poor Old Tom.'

In the woods at Ardo. Why did Moura say those words so often, on the evening of the day we'd been to Blackstone, as we sat in the dining-room so long that it grew dark and the candles too bright, holding all our eyes because we didn't want to look at each other? In the woods at Ardo Philip and I had made love for the first time. It was a hot summer evening and Moura was prowling in the kitchen garden, making sketches for a painting that would later show that moist, sun-melted place as hard and dry, jabbed with stiff fruit. It was the day after Philip asked me to marry him, in the boat under Cliff Hold. The leaves on the floor of the woods were dry and warm. We burrowed into them, like children trying to hide.

'I think a trip abroad would be a jolly good idea for you, Moura,' Sally said. There we were at the table, Gareth and Sally looking in at the walls where tapestries hung, Moura and I sitting together and looking across at them and beyond at the great purplish-blue haze of the sea. Sally was flushed with gin and her lipstick sat aslant her mouth. She waved her napkin as she talked. Twice Lily had come in to remove the plates and gone out again. Sally shovelled peas on to her fork and drew on a cigarette between forkfuls.

'I've too many things to attend to,' Moura said. *In the woods at Ardo* came the silent refrain between us. Philip pulled me so close in the leaves I thought I would suffocate. His hand went down to tug at my tights. My body ached with heat.

'The funeral's over,' Sally said in her no-nonsense voice. 'And I've got a surprise for you, Moura darling. I do hope you're pleased.'

'A surprise?' Moura said. The refrain started up again: *In the woods at Ardo.* Hugo walked slowly, carefully, in leaves of ten generations passing since I had lain there with his son. Who was he going to meet there? Why did he go alone?

'India,' Sally said. 'The Banglapores want you to stay. And Cutty's at the Bangkok embassy and longing for you to go on there.'

Moura looked vague. Her eyes were the same colour as the sea outside where it meets the sky. I was glad I wasn't walking in the garden, passing the window as Moura stared out. I could see myself frozen by the stare, turned to stone and falling on to the rocks below.

'You could do some marvellous painting in the East,' Sally said. She pushed away her plate and concentrated on the cigarette. It had tipped from the ashtray and left a brown snake on the dining table. Normally Moura would have been furious at that.

'It does sound a good idea, Moura,' Gareth said. It was the first time he'd spoken all evening. The fact he chose his first words to be words that encouraged his mother to leave her own home – and his possible protection – was embarrassing. Again, we all looked into the candle flames, which burnt more fiercely as they went down.

'I'm not interested in Oriental landscape,' Moura said. 'I'm finishing my series of paintings of the woods at Ardo.'

Silence again. I thought of Philip and I heard my cry of pain in the silence. I was so hot I could feel currents of cold air blow through the leaves where I was naked. Philip started to cry. His hair was wet in front. Then there was a shout, and his sudden falling back, as if he'd been knocked out into another world.

'My "Four Seasons",' Moura said. 'I'm waiting for autumn. The leaves are quite extraordinary – but you know, I want to try and paint them as Bonnard would have painted them. With passion' – her arm shot out and silver bangles crashed – 'and with vigour. Also,' she lowered the famous eyes, 'also, as a memorial.'

We were all stunned. I honestly don't think any of us had realized how strong Moura's obsession with the place had become. It explained, perhaps, Hugo's visit – she must after all have taken him there several times in the months of high summer.

'Is . . . was . . . did Hugo go very often to the . . . woods?' I forced myself to say. I saw Philip lying as if dead in leaves that were some of them still green and yellow and fallen for no apparent reason from the tree. I edged away from him. I was frightened by the instant, deathly sleep after love. 'Oh yes,' Moura said drily. 'Very often.'

Hugo picked his way through the trees with care but he wanted to be like a young man, to walk carelessly. A young woman with black hair was waiting for him in the middle of the woods. Kitty Rooney held her arms out to him laughing as he came close. Hugo was old, romantic, Yeats in old age. He laughed too and held out his arms in reply. He lurched; he tripped; he fell. They lay side by side, father and son, unmoving in the leaves.

Dinner that night seemed to go on for ever. When I look back on it now I see that it was because Sally ate so slowly, and the light faded so slowly; it was an evening in early autumn that lingers on like summer. I see the polished table and the candles reflected in the wood, tall and orange like the trees in the woods at Ardo. I spent most of that evening, in my most real memory, in those woods; the other happenings at Cliff Hold stand out like objects in a Dutch still-life: fish, silver and fresh from the sea; a shirt, crumpled; a child's face in the light from the door; and a drawer in the kitchen, a drawer in the dresser that wouldn't shut.

The fish came in a basket, slung on a canvas rope round the neck of a child. I was the one to go to the door when there was a knock – I was thankful to get away from the dining-room and the air of combined suspense and anti-climax that it was Moura's special genius to produce. Lily wasn't going to the door because as I went down the passage I heard her moving about in the kitchen. Perhaps she'd had enough of the day. I pulled open the big front door to Cliff Hold and looked out. The child gazed up at me. She held two mackerel in her left hand; with the right she fumbled at the catch of a canvas bag. 'Would Mrs Pierce buy the fish?' she said.

I recognized the child from Old Tom's garden earlier, but I didn't feel surprised – I didn't wonder how she'd come seven miles at night and was here now, holding fish still glistening from the sea. As in a dream, I accepted all this as quite natural. And it seemed natural too that the child showed no sign of recognizing me, although she'd held the horse for me only a few hours earlier.

'I don't know,' I said. 'I don't think Mrs Pierce will
. . .' Something in me had no wish to break the odd,
other dream that was passing in the dining-room,
Moura's dream in the woods that had everyone caught
in remembering. I didn't want to walk in, talk of
transactions of money and food.

'For God's sake,' the child said. 'Tell Mrs Pierce to
buy the fish.'

The urgent voice woke me and I turned and went
down the corridor sharply. I looked back once: there
was the pale face of the child, lit by the light from the
hall. It was finally dark outside. I went in: Gareth and
Sally and Moura were sitting in silence round the
candle-lit table. No one looked up as I came in,
although they must all have been listening to our
voices at the door.

'Moura,' I said, 'there's a child out there who wants
you to buy some mackerel.'

Moura rose. She was lit by the candles from below.
She looked like the Madonna they carry through the
streets in Spain: waxen, beautiful, calm.

'Very well,' Moura said. 'I'll go and see to it.'

Gareth half rose but her look made him sit down
again. 'Surely you don't need to buy fish at this hour of
night,' he said. Sally laughed at this. 'You've forgotten
what living in Ireland is, Gareth,' she said. 'People may
not come to your apartment door with mackerel in
New York but here . . .' She laughed again, to show
she bore Gareth no ill for not living in Ireland. And
Gareth pretended to join in, relieved, no doubt, to
return to the ordinary, while I stood, half in, half out of
the door, unable to make myself rejoin the table, and I
saw the fish, and the child's face – and then Moura
stooping over the child, helping her unfasten the
canvas bag.

118

Last night I shall think of as the night I realized I must go before it was too late. But it was too late, with the lateness of nightmare, the sense of time gone, flying out of sight and yet lurking there to be caught, like a slippery fish falling into a canvas bag. I rose and walked out into the passage, but like a sleepwalker I knew I wouldn't leave the house. I was stiff with fear but still I knew I was safe.

It must have been Moura who had left the lights on in the passage, because she was always the one to turn them off. I went down over the bumpy pebble mosaic and I felt my feet hurting, but a long way off, as if pain was taking a long time to get through. The lights in the passage were bright and white, like lights in a hospital.

I knew I wouldn't find Moura in the kitchen, but I knew she'd been there. The lights weren't on, though, and I had to grope for a switch. At my step, Philip's collection of junk from the Third World shifted on the top of the cabinet and the gourd fell, with a dry rattle, on to the lino. Moura wouldn't hear, up in her thick-walled room. She'd be pacing, waiting for Philip to come back, going to the window and looking out across the Atlantic. If Philip walked in now, he would walk across ten years and he and I could start in another way, in a time when Hugo never met Kitty Rooney, and Moura was always happy. In my fairy-tale dream, I went over to the dresser. What was happening wasn't happening, what could never happen might suddenly come true. I pulled open the drawer and put my hand on the bag.

Those were my dreams for the rest of the night: time, like a shadow that seemed to lie always in front of me on the lino floor as I stepped back from the dresser, and which then turned tail and fled after me down the corridor. In my hands I held a canvas fishing-bag. But in the bag the fish were long and hard.

Tuesday, September 3rd

Fran arrived yesterday. I couldn't believe it at first – she looked so exactly the same as when I'd known her – if anything more self-confident – and she smiled all the way through the first morning at Cliff Hold, as if she hadn't missed the funeral, as if Moura was really pleased to see her and as if she'd been longing to see me all these years. It's success, I suppose: in her office people smile back at her because she holds their lives in her hands. On location, when she drives up with her powerful equipment, victims of war-torn zones see their one way of making the world understand these terrible things that are happening to them. The heavy cameras are worth more than dollars. They smile if they can still smile at all, at the cool girl, as pretty as a picture in a Yankee magazine – the girl with the cameras and the long, dark hair.

The first trouble yesterday morning was occasioned by the cameras. Fran had left them in the hall (she hadn't brought the really large ones of course, but these looked as if they could shoot a pretty professional film) and Moura's flower basket was found flattened when she went out to pick flowers for the sitting-room. It was a long basket, with a falling-apart handle: I'd known it since I was a child and I felt a pang when it was pulled out from under the equipment, crushed and useless. Fran smiled through that as well.

'Oh, I'm sorry, Moura. I'll buy you another one. Do you find them in the . . .' she paused, trying to remember where in the world she was. 'In Cork? I'll go in tomorrow.'

'No, you can't get them there,' Moura said. She

spoke quietly, but I knew how angry she was. I wondered if I should take Fran aside and explain my fears for Moura.

'They must have *something* for flowers,' Fran said. 'Leave it to me.'

We all went out on to the lawn. We toured the staircase garden in silence. The sea was a perfect pale blue, the outline of the hills over the bay faint but definite. To anyone else the place would seem exotic, beautiful when seen through the tropical garden Moura had made as a frame. Anyone else would have exclaimed with pleasure and surprise – and many people did, when Moura led members of visiting botanical societies into her paradise filled with strange flowers and shrubs – she walking ahead and throwing back modest glances, the now defunct flower basket on her arm. Fran said nothing. Her thoughts appeared to be somewhere else. Her only apparent connection with Gareth was that they both wore identical American anoraks – a lumber-jack look, no doubt for wear at Fran's parents' estate in Martha's Vineyard. She walked briskly, Gareth trailed miserably after us.

'I wonder why you brought the cameras at all,' Moura said when we returned in embarrassing silence to the lawn by the sitting-room windows. Lacking a proper container, Moura had made Gareth hold the flowers she'd picked, and his hands were bleeding from thorny scratches. 'I mean, they must have been an awful bore in a plane and one can simply use one's eyes here I would have thought.'

Fran smiled. Any possibility of being accused of possessing the traits of a common tourist, of being able only to see life through the lens of a Polaroid camera, seemed not to occur to her. She answered earnestly, while maintaining the smile. 'Oh, I'm going to do something here,' she said. 'I just don't know whether I'll go up to the North or not, yet.'

'Do something?' Moura knew what she meant, I could see that, but she couldn't bear to believe it. I stood awkwardly between the daughter-in-law and the mother and wished I was the other side of the world. Gareth, muttering about the flowers, went in through the windows and started shouting to Lily for a vase. His petulant tone took me back to childhood once more. I could feel Moura praying for Fran never to have existed, to go away.

'Well . . . on Hugo,' Fran said. 'The circumstances of his death.'

Moura stared at Fran. There was nothing she could say, probably. But her powerlessness was so sudden it was pathetic. The cameras could invade her life, wreck it and leave again without a qualm. I saw the victim look on her face: she even tried to smile back at Fran.

'But what good would it do?' she asked. Her voice was mock-ingenuous, she was trying to charm with her quaint, old-fashioned lack of knowledge of modern technology. 'I mean – Hugo's dead and that's that.'

I wish you thought that, Moura, I said to myself. But before I had time to think more, I heard Fran delivering another bombshell as we went up the steps into the sitting-room. She stopped by the open windows. Gareth was pushing flowers into his mother's favourite vases and I heard Moura give a moan of anger and anxiety.

'The man on the run from the police,' Fran said. 'You call them the Guards here, right?'

'The man?' Moura repeated.

'The man they're looking for after that hotel bombing in Dongelly,' Fran said. 'Last news before I left said he was thought to be hiding out near here.'

'Gareth!' Moura shouted through the window. '*Leave those flowers! At once!*'

'Yeah, name Declan Rooney,' Fran went on with as little care for Moura's state as she would have had in the cutting-room for an unwanted clip of film. 'They said the Guards were on his trail and they even said – what's the name of the village down there?' We all looked down on Dunane, but no one spoke.

'Dunane,' said Fran, whose memory was essential to her success in her job. 'His family comes from there, at any rate. After lunch I'm going to go down and fix up an interview.'

We stood in silence. Then Fran started to make glowing remarks about Cliff Hold. It was too late, of course.

'It's so lovely here. So much more beautiful than Martha's Vineyard,' Fran said. And she meant it, one could see. And, as we went up into the sitting-room: 'Oh what fantastic colours, Moura.' And, turning to look back out at the stairs to the sea, the bay, the caravans carefully hidden by the palms, she did indeed seem to see the place for the first time. 'I'm *sorry*. I never made it here before. Now I see what I've been missing. I just got too tied up in work to come over.'

Moura and I looked out in absolute despondency at our beloved view from Cliff Hold. We saw it on an outsize TV, a set where the colours are Hawaiian-bright and dots dance in the sea and sky. We both saw it, I'm sure of that; the cameras tracking slowly to a wood. A man was walking, two men followed him. With the easy pointlessness of violence, Hugo fell and was dead.

It's hard to know how to describe the subtle changes in Fran since I last knew her more than ten years ago. She's more positive about herself, certainly – but I feel

123

a chilly undercurrent, which is all the stronger when you see her New York-career friendliness come up against the atmosphere at Cliff Hold. She seems to be wrapped in a permanent cellophane. The enthusiasm and easy-success aura which had so impressed me at film school are still there, but they've solidified, hardened: if you walk ahead of her and look round suddenly the smiling face has gone and a calculating, cautious look sits there instead. It must be hard to get to the top of a job like hers – and keep it, while being a feminist and a serious, politically committed person as well.

We were very glad to see each other, though. Fran half lay across my bed, like she used to do in my mother's dinky mews house. Her long, black hair was shining, almost blue; here and there was a white strand, ridiculous, I thought at first, she's too young – but the white hairs are a reminder that even someone like Fran is human, ages like any other animal. Otherwise she's still the 'new species', the new New Woman. I was dignified, reticent with her at first. But Fran can drag anything out of anyone.

'Wow, it's great to be here,' she said, and reached out to pat my shoulder. 'Funny how we never thought ten years ago we'd end up in a remote corner of Ireland together.' She laughed.

I was the one who wanted to get news from Fran, at first. But I was shy about asking her questions. So I waited, while Fran expounded on her general amazement at the eccentricities of Cliff Hold. 'I mean, someone built this dump to *live in*,' she said. 'Suitable for the Man in the Iron Mask, no mod cons, impossible to escape.' Fran was in good form, evidently. I felt the smell of Manhattan streets, the laughter at parties when she gets back and tells of Ireland and Cliff Hold.

'Of course, your family never liked Ireland, did

they?' I said. I wanted to warn Fran: be careful what you knock, over here.

'That wouldn't bias me,' Fran said in a sudden, sharp professional voice. She slid off the bed and sat cross-legged on the floor. 'Tell me, Minnie, what the hell is going on here. I don't want to be naive, but it looks as if things aren't right. Or is that just the natural hatred of a woman for her daughter-in-law?'

'Oh I'm sure she doesn't hate you . . . ' I began.

'She wants me out of here as fast as she can get me,' Fran said. 'Is there something fishy with Hugo's death? There are hints in the States, you know – "Twice-nominated Nobel author found dead in Irish wood", that kind of thing.'

'I – I just don't know Fran,' I said. I sounded feeble, even to myself. 'I think Moura ought to go away for a break. The whole thing's made her rather . . . '

How awful to be English! My words sounded like a prep school report on the last day of summer term when the games didn't go very well.

Fran looked up at me with that sharp look again. 'She's out of her mind, Minnie, if you ask me. That performance with the shirt at lunch. Is this what you've been living with since you came over?'

You might think that Fran's words came as a blast of fresh air after the claustrophobia of the last days with Moura. But I felt only confused by them; miserable; why didn't she resume her global tours of violence and leave me and Moura here alone together, in our own little world? Fran decided to zoom in on Cliff Hold and her eyes, with the impassivity of a camera, recorded it and probed its secret life. I suppose she had had a bad time, meeting such a wall of hostility. But she wasn't going to imagine that her own refusal to come over in the past, her holding Gareth back from his mother, hadn't caused the silent disapproval of Moura. 'I don't

125

truck with female politics,' Fran said later when I broached the subject. And that was that. Now, we both sat in silence and pondered the episode of the shirt.

It was lunch – or rather it was coffee after lunch – that had prompted Moura to get up suddenly and go out of the room. She'd put a white cloth on the table and some of her coffee had spilled – I think her hands were shaking too much to hold a cup properly. Fran and Gareth and I looked at each other without betraying a thing. Lily came in, saw the coffee stain and made a clicking sound. We went on sitting in silence.

'Moura's not herself at the moment,' Gareth said in a colourless voice. I wasn't sure whom he was telling: Fran, who hadn't seen her mother-in-law, presumably, for some years, or me, both an intimate and a stranger.

'Can we go down and interview some inhabitants of Dunane?' Fran said briskly. 'I'd like to get something on film before evening.'

Gareth directed a hopeless look in the direction of Fran. I could see him suffer at the thought of the private places of his childhood, the people he'd always known in Dunane, exposed on screens all over the world. He must, too, after a strained lunch that had been as bad as the guided tour of the garden, suffer at the fact that Fran and Moura just can't bear each other. Or did he, I wondered, as he sat on, crumbling bread into pellets on the cloth, did he care about anything now? Had life in New York done this to him – given him absolute nullity? Or was it Fran, powerful and always right, using the tools of feminism when she needed to get her way? Perhaps guilt, and relative failure compared with Fran's career, fear of a rootless future, had made Gareth like this. Is he even able to remember his childhood here – Hugo – anything? Or am I just unable to see him clearly? (It's said that women writing about men make them shadowy, unbelievable figures, whether they're powerful or weak. Is that because men live in so different a world that women find it hard to imagine? Or are women really more interested in themselves?)

'What was the name of that woman who sent us those catastrophic hunting prints as a wedding present?' Fran said. 'I'll go see her.'

I saw Gareth hesitate. Fran's nose for the right contact had proved true, as usual. He looked, desperately this time, across at me.

'She must have been at the funeral,' Fran said. 'Come on, Minnie, you can't have forgotten her name.'

'Sally,' I said. It is impossible to disobey Fran.

'Oh right. And where does she live?' A small notebook had popped out of the folds of Fran's fashionable-length skirt. A thin gold pencil rose in the air at the ready.

I gave the address, as far as I could remember it. And I had to add – it's as if the giving of directions has its own hidden rules: 'You can't miss it. When you leave Dunane you take the road out to Ballinstrae. It's a big white house behind gates on the left, just by the turning off to Ardo.'

Moura came in, of course, just as I said the word. She gave me a look of pure panic. I wanted to say, I wasn't betraying you, Moura. I promise I wasn't. But I couldn't say anything. Moura put a white bundle she was carrying down on the table.

'Now I want you to look at this,' she said.

Fran half rose: the sight of anything so domestic as household linen probably set off a flight mechanism. I thought it must be another example of spilled coffee. Moura wasn't like this normally – whatever her strangenesses, she'd never shown obsession with table-cloths, sheets: anything like that she pushed off on to Lily. Perhaps the startling career of a younger woman had made her retreat into a motherly, fussy-hen role, her own career as a painter parochial and dim in comparison.

'You can see what happened,' Moura said.

We all gaped at the shirt – it was a white shirt, well made like all Hugo's clothes. What had looked like another example of a coffee stain was in fact two great splotches of mud, roughly circular, on the back below the shoulder blades.

'They threw stones,' Moura said.

This time Gareth rose to his feet. He reached out for the shirt, but Moura pulled it back. 'Didn't you show that to the Guards?' he said. His white face had gone red in spots.

'They don't count it,' Moura said in a voice that was quiet and sweet, like an actress imitating a secretary questioned by her boss. 'They say it's just a dirty shirt.'

'And he was definitely wearing it, that . . . day?'

'Oh no. I invented the whole thing,' Moura said in a sudden blaze of anger. Then quiet and reasonable again: 'Of course he was, Gareth. It was a beautiful, warm day. He didn't take a jacket. He went for a walk in the woods at Ardo.'

'I almost have the feeling,' Fran said as we sat in my room, 'that Moura wants Gareth to carry out some kind of vengeance for her.' Fran shook her head in a kind of mock admiration. 'I've been to some strange locations – the Yoruba women were incredible, what they'd come to expect of fathers and husbands – but this has a primaeval touch. Was she always like this, Minnie?'

'I . . . I think she minds very much about Hugo,' I said.

'Mm.'

Fran isn't interested in love relationships. I felt a stirring pity for Gareth. 'I'm sure she wouldn't want Gareth to do anything dangerous,' I reassured her.

'You can't mean you take it seriously?' Fran sat up straight on the floor and looked at me as if I might be worth making a film study of. 'Who are these "they" anyway? Envious authors? Mexican revolutionaries who didn't like the tone of the last book?'

'Not exactly,' I said. 'I'm not sure.'

'You wouldn't go far as a journalist,' Fran said with that same open smile. 'I'll find out for myself, then.'

'Yes. But – Fran . . . ' I didn't know how to use her language when I was at Cliff Hold. Here, everything seems possible, while in Fran's studio and editing room the mystery and possibilities are taken out of life and one side is shown as the truth. 'I'm just saying, be careful about Gareth and Moura,' I said.

Fran whistled. 'Beware,' she said. 'Minnie, you're just as much of a dope as you always were. But you're still as sweet. What do I have to be careful of?'

'Gareth's in a bit of a strung-out state.' I tried to sound cool. 'I mean, Moura might – might get him to do something he'd regret.'

Fran was silent. She seemed embarrassed for me. I suddenly heard myself break the silence with the question I'd promised myself I wouldn't ask. 'How's Philip?' I said. 'Oh Fran, it would be so much better if he could be over here now.'

Fran's look changed to pity. Even in her busy life she must have thought of the irony of our old friendship: my visit to New York when I was on top of the world, engaged to marry Philip, and she hadn't even met Gareth. But there is no irony, in fact: my having lost Philip means nothing to her. How much I've thought about her over the years, though, with Philip her

129

brother-in-law in New York, getting to know him probably in a way she would think was superior to my way of knowing him. Though that could never be.

'He's fine – been away lately,' Fran said. Her smile grew more determined. She's trying to hide something, I thought.

'Of course, one does hear the odd thing about him in London.' My worldly tone, taken from aged and drunken literary friends of my mother's, failed to impress, I could see. 'Still going out with the smart and wealthy young ladies of the metropolis,' I went hideously on. 'It seems rather a shame he couldn't bring himself to come over for the funeral. He and Hugo were terribly close once, you know. Oh yes.' I settled on the bed, cheeks aflame with the horror of my tone, which had turned by now into something old-retainer-like. 'They never spent a moment apart when he was a child. Even as a young man Philip was influenced entirely by Hugo. Whatever happened I'd have thought he'd be here.'

Fran got up and went over to the window. It was an overcast afternoon and the great distance, the sense of energy and activity she brought with her made the time until dark unbearably long. I saw myself at the airport – my arrival in Kennedy – the first bite of autumn in the air, and maybe a loft where I could pursue my artistic activities. Philip came to pick me up in a cab. We went to a glittering party and then on out to supper. We went back to his apartment, which had serious lamps to help him read all the millions of words he had to digest and review. And we kissed on a leather sofa – Philip had taken it from Cliff Hold when he left. ('Yes, you can have that,' Hugo'd said . . . The sofa was his favourite piece in his study, so it showed how much he loved Philip and how high his hopes were for him. Lily pulled a face at all the dust on the floor where it had stood.)

'The truth is,' said Fran, who was standing at the window with her back to me, 'I don't know where he is.'

'What?' I goggled up at her. That had never occurred to me – nor had it occurred to Moura, I'm sure. Then I remembered why not. 'He sent a cable,' I said. 'It came from Washington.'

'Yes,' said Fran. 'But I sent that, you see. So it's not much help.'

'You sent it?'

'Philip doesn't know Hugo's dead. Maybe he does now, with all the press coverage. But probably only just. I sent the cable to . . . to spare Moura's feelings. I guess he's in a very remote spot.'

'Like the Falklands?' I saw Philip mud-blackened and brave, reporting a war. That wasn't his usual line of business, it was true, but he probably felt he spent too much time away from the action.

'Not exactly.' Fran's smile seemed completely real and unforced. 'More comfortable than that, I'd say. He got married, you see. It must've been about a fortnight ago. He said he was going down to somewhere near Samoa on honeymoon.'

I don't want to be unkind to Fran. Perhaps I'm less impressed by her than I was ten years ago – but she is fearless in a way that's attractive. She's uncompromising. I like the way she thinks she can wrap up the world and shoot it out by satellite like a gift-wrapped package. It's naive, perhaps, in a very American way. Yet she hasn't the European cynicism and despair. She believes strongly in what she does. I know that's what really counts.

I'm just putting this down to steady myself before I

think back on yesterday afternoon – the last hours before the light began to fade – when Fran, after walking casually out of my room, picked up her camera equipment from the hall and loaded it into the boot of the car (a blue Ford Escort, like Gareth's) also hired at the airport. The engine started and a string of cats ran out from under the wheels. I stood at my window a few minutes before I went out into the drive, and by that time the car was going down the lane. The figure of Moura was just visible on the left-hand side of the road, under the purple-red hedges. The car didn't slow down; Fran didn't poke her head out of the window to ask if Moura wanted a lift. Moura didn't look at the car or wave.

Thursday, September 5th
Confusion – and, worst of all, a certainty growing up through the confusion: the certainty that Moura will do anything and will stop at nothing; that she is sewn into the past here at Cliff Hold as firmly as the figures in the tapestry and that law, time, reason, mean nothing to her any more. Monday and Tuesday built up together into a horrific symphony of her cunning, her melodrama, her longing for violence. Yesterday was calm – but it's a calm that would deceive no one. She's still the Moura I love – it's just that some of the strands in her have come apart: she no longer makes up a whole. On Monday when Moura set off down the lane on foot, I knew she must be going to the field – the other side of the road and rented to her by the Ryans – where she keeps the horses. I knew she was going to ride over to Blackstone. Sure enough, she was back late for dinner and Lily was scowling in the kitchen. It was nearly dark outside. Moura had that strange, rapt expression which made Gareth so uncomfortable he

couldn't look. Fran was careful not to make trouble by revealing her own activities of the afternoon. It was left to me to make conversation to Moura, to try and talk of anything that didn't lead back to the woods at Ardo.

Everything did, of course. Fran mentioned she'd been for 'a little drive' (she'd been to Sally's: with a sinking heart I made that out) and at first she'd almost taken the wrong turning, instead of going off in the direction of Ardo. A stony silence met this remark. She'd filmed some of the beautiful countryside. Another silence. And so on. But somehow we got through the meal and went off to our separate rooms, Moura climbing to her upper bedroom with a weary but triumphant air and Gareth going into his room and slamming the door in exasperation. Fran said she'd like to come and sit with me, but I said I was tired. I needed the time, I suppose, to digest the news she'd brought as well as try to think what is going to happen here, if Moura goes on in this way.

I needn't have wasted time and thought on it. Moura and Fran, like two sides of a dress that has split apart, are blown by their desires and ambitions along paths that have always lain in wait for them. It's as if their natures, enormously magnified, lurk in every tree and cloud; the landscape is one minute Moura's and the next it is Fran's.

Nor did I need to think that my telling Fran I was tired was going to make the slightest difference. People in her world are never tired. I heard her clump over the pebble floor of the passage and I watched the door-handle turn. Fran came in.

'Minnie,' she said.

There was no need to answer, either. Fran's eyes were shining – like they used to shine when she was first at film school – when she came into my room late at night to tell me of a new piece of film technique she thought she'd made up all by herself.

'I think I've got something!' She settled on the floor, long hair swinging shut over her face. She pushed it back and looked up at me. 'Sally – Sally Balmartin. When I went to see her she more or less made it clear that *everyone* here is covering up for the Rooneys. And I see what she means – *everyone* I talked to in Dunane had seen them *somewhere* on the morning Hugo died.'

'Oh,' I said. I thought of the lunging figure under the car, the rage of the man in the group in the lane by the white shoebox houses. I saw his rage again, from the rear window of the funeral car – and for some reason I heard my mother – who can she have been talking about? – say, 'Oh he's got a terrible Paddy'. I saw a hand raised and Hugo fall. Did rage make killing more forgivable?

'She told me she wanted the whole thing forgotten as quickly as possible,' Fran said. 'She wants to take Moura round the world or something. You know, they may have been lovers once!'

I looked down from my bed at Fran on the floor and I laughed. She couldn't get things right, somehow. Yet once I had thought she was right about everything.

'And I went to the *Cork Examiner.* They put me on to the detective agency Hugo hired to follow Des Rooney. Guy there says he's going to take me tomorrow to the apartment where he believes Des and his brother Declan did more than just store stolen VTRs, TVs and the like. He believes there may be a cache . . . since the Dongelly hotel incident . . .'

'Fran,' I said, 'don't you think it's time to go to bed?'

I knew as I spoke that I was being everything Fran despised – I was utterly English – I was hiding my head in the sand. Hugo despised that in people, too.

'You're just like Sally Balmartin,' Fran said in predictable contempt. 'She wants everything – always – to stay the same.'

And Hugo laughed at Sally for that in his books, I thought, as Fran rose and went yawning ostentatiously to the door. But in his own life he liked 'everything to stay the same' – and so, in all truth, does Fran.

Tuesday morning I rose early because I could sense the currents of violent intention in the house: even the orange cats outside my window were more than usually vicious and I was woken by hissing and spitting on the ledge. I lay for a while staring at the tapestry. But the action had moved off the walls and into the house. Doors opened and shut and a gust of wind came into the hall from what must have been an open door. Who was going where at this hour of the morning? Then I heard the car start up and I knew Fran had gone.

Moura didn't come into the dining-room for breakfast. I found her in the kitchen, talking in a low, fast voice to Lily, a cup of tea slopping over in her hand. She looked up and was quite surprised to see me, as if she'd forgotten I'd come to stay.

'Ah, Minnie.'

'Moura.' I went up to her but she wouldn't meet my eyes. 'How . . . how are you this morning?' I said. I knew I sounded foolish; both Moura and Lily looked at me with that familiar look.

'I'm just discussing the food for the next few days,' Moura said in a dismissive tone. 'I must go down to Ryan's.'

'I'll come with you,' I said.

'There's no point,' Moura said, a little too quickly.

'You'll do better to help me here,' Lily said. 'There's all the beds and I'll never get home at this rate.'

'Home?' I said. The change of direction had worked. 'When are you going home, Lily?'

'I'm going over . . . ' Lily began.

'Lily *must* go to Blackstone on Saturday,' Moura said. 'It's the Ballinstrae Games. You hadn't forgotten, had you, Minnie?'

'Oh no,' I said, 'of course not.' I had; but the mention of the Games brought back all the years when I used to come here: the people on the road to the abbey at Blackstone; and Philip and I when we were small being allowed to watch from the branches of the yew tree outside the door of the old house. I smelt the September morning with the nose of childhood. Lily and Old Tom came from their half-in, half-out cottage with jugs of Guinness and lemonade and cakes studded with currants. On the sunken lawns children hopped three-legged and ran balancing china eggs. A band played: once in the kitchen garden I'd seen one of the bandsmen taking a pee up against the raspberry canes.

'I went over yesterday,' Moura said. 'To make some preparations. Cousin Henry and Cousin Ottoline don't go to any trouble. In my mother's day there was everything – country dancing, pony rides – even a fortune teller in a tent.'

I'd heard the speech countless times. A wave of homesickness for the past came over me. I saw Moura pottering cheerfully on the lawn yesterday afternoon as she has always done, laying out stakes for the relay race and moving, with the help of the ancient gardeners, the trestle tables and upturned tubs where jumble and teas will be laid out. But in the past she didn't come back from these excursions with a strange, glittering air – as if she'd found a clairvoyant after all and had heard deathly news. And the gardeners – in my mind's eye they changed from innocent old men to Moura's conspirators: what had they been doing at Blackstone yesterday afternoon?

'The birds are taking all that's left of the blackcurrants in the kitchen garden,' Moura said. 'It's shocking. I decided it was time something was done about it.'

But I was too deep in memory of childhood expeditions to Blackstone to pick up the tone in Moura's voice. Instead, I crawled under nets in the sticky heat. Philip nudged me as we followed Moura's torn cotton skirt. We heaved with giggles. Moura held the basket: first the strawberries, on straw that was always damp from rain, then gooseberries, then blackcurrants so tart we spat them out. Philip and I came bump up against Moura when she stopped in her tracks and we burst into giggles again.

'I'm sure Philip will be here in time for the Games,' Moura said, picking up my thoughts and speaking in her new, odd 'serene' voice. 'It'll be lovely, won't it, Minnie?'

I stared at the cabinet, with the photograph of Gareth and Fran on their wedding day. Gareth faces the camera – he is neutralized by his years in America, homogenized and plasticked, a man of no particular nationality who has just married a rich, successful American woman. For the first time I felt Moura's impatience with him myself. Maybe all she wants from Gareth is some loyalty, some memory of family ties stronger than credit cards.

Moura turned to Lily and picked up a list from the top of the cabinet. She read from the list: ham; tomatoes; potatoes. All right Lily, Persil, I heard you the first time. (And I watched Gareth come into the kitchen, in response to Moura's call.) 'Yes, the Games'll be the day, surely it will,' Lily said, as she said every year, and I felt the excitement I used to feel as a child, before Hugo 'opened' the fete, as he liked to call it. (He thoroughly enjoyed his masquerade of squirearchy on his wife's estates.) Gareth didn't look at

137

Moura, just stood with his pale head down and staring gloomily at the kitchen floor. Moura went up to him, using a cheer-up voice that clearly grated on him.

'I was saying, Gareth, that I'm sure you'll take Lily over to Blackstone on Saturday. It's the Games, you know. And she hasn't been home for days. Old Tom must be missing her. So you'll take her, I hope?'

'Sure,' Gareth said.

'That'll be great,' Lily said. An air of cosiness settled between Moura and Lily and I tried to recapture that safe mood of the past, when a small plan was success-fully negotiated. But I saw only Old Tom gyrating like a madman in the cabbage patch, and a dog running barking to the gap in the wall that leads on to the hill of Ardo. Gareth shuffled his feet. He was anxious to be gone.

'Just help me with the order at Ryan's, will you, darling?' Moura said. 'So much heavy stuff and it's rather a crowded day for Mr Ryan to try to carry it all out.'

Gareth shrugged, nodded, and walked to the door. I said, thinking of Moura and the Games, 'But Moura, aren't you going over to Blackstone on Saturday in the car? I mean . . . can't we go together and take Lily . . .'

'Oh no, Gareth must take Lily,' Moura said. 'See you later, Minnie dear.'

Clasping a large, black shopping-bag, Moura went out into the hall. I went to the kitchen door and called after her.

'Can't I help carry too, Moura? Really?'

'No, Minnie. We'll be quite all right as we are.' Moura's voice was firm.

I waited a few minutes, chatting to Lily as she peeled potatoes at the sink, before setting off down to Ryan's, in the main street at the end of the fuchsia lane.

138

It's impossible not to remember Fran on her return from her next great 'investigative' trip – impossible not to wonder how she could be so blind as to fail to see the state I was in, after the horrors of the morning, the débâcle in Ryan's shop, the sensation, as happens in times of stress, of months having passed since we all left the house earlier that day. But then Fran's sensitivity has gone into film – or so she would like to think. In fact, under the guise of 'getting to grips with things' and 'detachment' and all the rest, she simply takes very little in.

'Minnie, it's just too much to find a world like this still going on in the modern age,' Fran said, after bursting into my room and finding me lying on my bed. My head and eyes ached. The tapestry, with its figures on horses stepping delicately through the woods, was hazy and dark.

'Sally,' Fran expounded. 'She's another time. It's like – like the Tale of Genji – ' she pointed at the tapestry, 'like that. The court of Diane de Poitiers or something. I told her she must get in touch with the police – she's so feudal, though, I suppose she imagines a private army from somewhere will turn up and put everything straight.'

'What?' I half sat, then sank back again. Fran's cheeks were tinged with healthy colour. Her black hair stuck out like a gigantic shadow round her head: I don't remember when I've seen her so dishevelled. She's excited, I thought, with that numb feeling coming back again.

'Sally knows the corruption of local politics round here,' Fran said. 'She knows that nothing's being done now because Des Rooney is close with Ryan and Ryan is close with Johnny Oge . . . '

I closed my eyes. Something that is private – to Moura – to me – to Philip – was being turned into a film documentary. I saw Johnny Oge talking to Fran: his expansive smile and his defence of the Rooneys. His fingers spread out as he talked. I saw Sally, in the good-taste interior of her mock-Gothic house, leaning forward in a needlework chair and saying to Fran, 'Poor Hugo. He hated violence, you know. Des Rooney was a . . . well . . . a petty crook and a . . . wife batterer, if that's what they're called nowadays. Hugo was right to get a private detective on to him. But unfortunately one can't say he lived to regret it.'

Fran settled herself on the floor. Her heavy bags of film equipment were beside her. There was a sound of unzipping. I kept my eyes shut. But the film that played behind my eyes was as bad as the film I knew Fran wanted to show me. Stereotypes gestured and spoke to camera with insincerity. Every point was too simple, but conclusive. Why can't Fran leave all this alone? It's so much more complicated than it seems.

Ryan's. Somehow I walked past the white houses in the fuchsia lane and down to the corner. I turned left opposite Ryan's pub.

It was crowded in the shop and I went in unnoticed. The shop is crammed with plastic buckets and T-shirts and sandals in cellophane bags and kitchen equipment and cheap fishing-rods painted a metallic green – and dolls with white-blonde hair and buckets for fancy sandcastles – and all this before you even get to the counters that sell the serious stuff: bacon on the slicer all day long, great trays of sausages and butter and special offer chutney and pickles and jam. I made my way through an overhang of butterfly nets and mops to the centre of the shop. The main counter runs along here. Huge boxes of assorted chocolates block the view from the door of the shop. Behind the counter is the door Mr and Mrs Ryan slip in and out of – to the back room where the wives of Dunane meet for lemonade and cakes and a talk, and where the Ryans go to make their phone calls (they rent out boats, run two taxis, talk to farmers to whom they let out land). I pushed my way to the main counter, because it's where Moura always goes. She can wave at the re- frigerator and ask to see the pork. Or she can pick up a 'luxury item', sniff with contempt and lay it down.

The Rooneys were standing to the right of the main counter. There was a wedding cake behind them, with a tiny bridal couple hand-in-hand on the top. They stood obviously unknowing in front of this happy scene and they stared at the other couple by the counter – four or five feet down, I suppose. The couple was Gareth and Moura.

'Now can I help you?' Mr Ryan said.

No one moved. Mr Ryan darted two smiles – one deferential to Moura and Gareth, the other sly. 'You'll be looking forward to the Games, then,' he said, using the sly smile. The larger of the two Rooneys put his hand on the counter. The hand was as solid as a ham.

'We'll be there,' he said.

Mr Ryan moved back to Moura, head down in anticipation of her order.

When I opened my eyes, Fran had fixed up her video on the floor of my room. It was odd at first to see Sally small and brightly-coloured: the muted tones of her floral summer dress were lost on video. But her voice was horribly near, as if she'd come into the room to give me and not Fran an interview.

'The trouble with Hugo was that he got mixed up in the sordid side of things. If you know what I mean. I mean, Moura isn't exactly the femme fatale type – too head-in-the-clouds. Well, when this woman Kitty Rooney got bashed around by her husband, he took it too hard. I mean, she might've been enjoying it secretly, you know.' Sally's eyes blazed. She disappeared off the tiny screen to pour herself a gin – you could hear the glug from the bottle. Then she came back again. There was a silence while she fitted a cigarette into a long tortoiseshell holder. 'You never know with these people. Of course Rooney was a crook – no doubt about it. But nothing very exaggerated – Hugo should've left well alone.'

'You say there's another brother? Can you tell us anything about him?'

Fran's professional-interviewer American voice produced first a hiccup of disapproval, then silence. Then, 'Look, I know absolutely nothing about this at all. As I first told you, my dear.'

Fran switched off the machine. She beamed up at me, as if she had something so wonderful to tell that I must count myself lucky to be the first to hear it.

'Minnie,' she said. 'I found about the other brother. Declan Rooney. It *is* the guy who's suspected of being involved in the hotel bombings in Dongelly. You know.'

Oh, how Fran loves terrorism! Does she think she's coming close to revolution, like when she goes to the Gambia or El Salvador? Is this Rooney brother already a hero? I saw her eyes shine and I looked away.

'You see what a story this is,' Fran said. 'I'm going to call N.A.B. The great writer Hugo tied up with all this. It'll cause anti-Irish feeling just about the time they're all demonstrating in San Francisco in front of the Queen. It may make a difference to the election.'

'Wait a minute, Fran,' I said.

'But can't you see, Minnie?' Fran came right up to the edge of the bed, on her knees like she did when we were young, kneeling on the carpet in my mother's

142

mews house. 'Can't you see? There's been a murder here. I'm going to investigate. Sally doesn't have the right to keep her suspicions to herself.'

I shrank back. The orange cats started their mewing out in the garden. Where was Lily? It was getting dark. Where were Moura and Gareth? But I knew the answer to that: after leaving Ryan's they'd gone to the beach, to 'recover calm'. Where was Lily, though? The cats would have to be fed.

'You must have thought there'd been a murder before this,' I said. 'After all, Moura showed you that shirt.'

'I put it down to hysteria,' Fran said. 'Now I don't.' The film of Sally came to an end. Fran's long fingers searched in the bag. 'There's an interview with Johnny Oge I want to show you. And a surprise – the thing every reporter dreams of.' Fran gave me that incredibly generous, open smile again. 'I'll show you them both, Minnie. Then judge for yourself.'

Show me the face of the beast. Des Rooney has a bloated face, lively eyes, thick straight black hair which looks as if it's been sculpted into the same position for years. He has thick lips – but none of this means anything – it's the way he stands, head thrust forward, half-crouched, like a boxer. Aggression pours out of him; and to match it there's a loud laugh: the kind of laugh men make in bars when they're deprived of female company. He was wearing a jacket in a bright tweed. His brother was a smaller version of himself. Behind them on the rack hung the face of a girl who looks like their sister – on the cover of a magazine.

I don't know how the fight started, but now I look back I see with horrible clarity that Moura must have been responsible. It all seemed to happen so quickly:

143

one minute Mr Ryan was looking from Moura and Gareth to the Rooneys – he was uncomfortable, certainly, for he didn't know who had appeared at the counter to be served first – and the next, Moura had dropped what looked like a bundle of dirty washing. Des Rooney was jostled (it must have been Moura, circling the shop, coming up suddenly behind him); and both Rooneys closed up to Gareth at the counter. I was very near them now. The smell of Des Rooney's haircream made me sick. The smaller brother, whose face was thinner, sharper, more calculating, deliberately dug his elbow into Gareth's side.

'You're standing on something of mine!' Moura's voice was loud and high. Under the hanging paraphernalia other customers turned and looked. 'Mr Ryan!' Moura said. 'Will you please ask this customer to move!'

I didn't blame Mr Ryan. He turned with an instinctive gesture to the door of the back room behind him.

'Get off at once!' Moura caught her breath so noisily that a woman by the cooked-meat display tugged her two children out to the street. 'That's Mr Pierce's shirt!'

'Mrs Pierce. Please,' said Mr Ryan, who stood with his hand on the knob of his sanctuary door. 'Can we have a little less disturbance, please!'

I should have guessed what had inadvertently 'fallen to the floor' or had been apparently dropped there. I should have known, when I said Moura would stop at nothing, that she would be able to go as far as this in her determination to extract an 'honourable' vengeance from poor Gareth. She stooped, she tugged at the white shirt now grimy with the dirt of Ryan's floor. The shirt came away from under Des's feet with a tearing sound. He lunged forward, missing Moura, and punched Gareth straight under the right ear. And

Moura held up the shreds of linen like a flag: the muddy patches where Hugo had been hit by earth and stones waved over her head like an insignia of revenge.

Gareth's mouth began to bleed. He lurched out of the shop like a drunk, with Mr Ryan following behind and holding out his hands.

'You know who that is,' Fran said. We'd watched a short interview with Johnny Oge, where he produced exactly the same speech and winning mannerisms as he'd done with me after the funeral party. Now there was a red-haired man on the video. His face was instantly disturbing: like someone you know but it can't be.

'It's Charlie Grogan,' Fran said. 'Remember?'

'Charlie Grogan?' I thought. Oh God I remember he was a wild boy who used to go out and show Philip and me how to put down lines for lobsters. I'd forgotten him – why? For the same reasons, no doubt, as Gareth had forgotten me.

'He looks so old,' I said, foolishly. He must be my age, of course.

'That morning it was stormy all right.' Charlie Grogan was answering the invisible, persistent Fran. 'Won't forget that morning for the reason I'd been out on the sea all night!'

There was something about Charlie Grogan that I did remember suddenly. He was 'driven', in some way: he came close many times, with his suicidal feats of bravery, to ensuring the deaths of all three of us – Philip, me, himself. We didn't know the bravery was suicidal at the time – children seldom recognize these things – but whenever a big sea got up, a look of rare happiness would come into Charlie's eyes and he'd head out to sea with both of us too afraid to be thought cowards to ask him to turn back. I shuddered,

145

remembering the waves as they poured over us and the time we'd been washed up on the rocks under Cliff Hold in our life jackets and half-paralysed with cold.

'Worst night of my life,' Charlie said. His eyes lit up for a moment. (You might say a lot of these exploits came from a boy of Charlie's intelligence seeing the prospects for a boy in that fast-depopulating and declining part of the country, and there being no choice other than acts of unconscious self-destruction.) Now his eyes settled into gloom again. 'If it hadn't a' been for Mr Ryan on the beach there and he saw me and came out in his twin-diesel, I'd not have got home.'

'And that was the morning Mr Pierce was found dead, you're certain.'

'Sure I'm certain. I went up to Mrs Pierce's with the lobsters. Well, you never know at this time of year when she mightn't need them for a party. Oh it was a terrible thing, none of us even knowing Mr Pierce was dead and there I was standing with the lobsters and one of them wriggling half-way out of the basket.'

'And why do you remember that morning – I mean, after you'd been rescued and you'd gone up to Cliff Hold with the lobsters?'

Charlie Grogan blinked into camera. He must have sensed Fran's question was important, but couldn't for the life of him think why.

'I got a ride home,' he said. 'With Mr Ryan and Mr Oge. I told you that before.'

'You live near Blackstone, don't you?'

'Not too far.'

'And you stopped for two men just under Ardo. Two men on the road.'

'Sure we did.'

'And Mr Ryan and Mr Oge asked them to get in and

146

said they'd run them down to Dunane when they'd dropped you off.'

'Yes.' Charlie Grogan began to look uneasy. 'I told you they were the Rooney brothers,' he said. 'What's wrong with saying that?'

'There's nothing wrong with it,' Fran's voice came over on a note of triumph. 'Can you tell us what kind of a state they were in?'

'State?' Charlie Grogan looked bewildered. Fran laughed and turned off the video, so there was the eerie sound of her double laughter, recorded and real. She sat back on her knees and beamed up at me. 'You see, Minnie, we have something concrete to go on now. If I hadn't found Charlie Grogan – and he'd been out on a long fishing trip since the day after Hugo was killed – we'd never know this. Johnny Oge may say Des Rooney would never kill a man – but they were there, Minnie – the Rooneys were at Ardo that day. We can open up the case now!'

Dawn, Friday, September 6th:
Ah Fran, if only I felt you'd be able to get somewhere with your investigations! But I don't see how you can. Cliff Hold isn't just another underdeveloped part of the world waiting to be exploited by your cameras. This is Moura's home – and my home – and Philip's too, of course. He'll be back soon. After what you've told me, I don't doubt his return. I only wish I'd known then what I know now – how differently I'd have acted. We'd be married, living here happily: our marriage wouldn't be a travesty, like yours and Gareth's.

I had to hide a smile all the same, when Gareth lost his temper last night. I didn't find the strained atmosphere at dinner any more bearable than you did – but I don't get up and walk out of meals like you. I would never have shown those stupid little films of yours, either, on a night when everyone's nerves were at breaking-point. Of course you must have known Moura would put her head round the door of your room, just as you were showing your prize sequence: the film of Kitty Rooney coming out of her parents-in-law's white box of a house – Kitty Rooney seeing the cameras and Kitty Rooney pulling her black headscarf down over her face. So what is so special about that? It's just a persecuted young woman trying to hide. And how clever your timing was, to show that film when Moura was bound to notice that you weren't coming back into the dining-room and would come looking for you.

It was interesting, though, to see your reaction to Gareth's rage – when Moura was standing in your room and staring with dead eyes at the video of Kitty Rooney – I don't think I've ever seen her eyes go like that before – and you started up again in your 'reporter's voice'. You said you'd been in to Cork and gone to the newspaper office and they'd directed you to the private detective agency Hugo used for tracking down the activities of Des Rooney. (There are no boundaries for you, Fran, no private territory. No private relationships either – afraid of being trapped with the responsibilities of being a woman, you've left yourself with no sense of responsibility at all.)

'I'm sorry for Des Rooney,' Fran said. 'I mean, he was totally persecuted by that agency, you know.'

Gareth was sitting on the end of the bed. Moura still stood against the door. The video now showed views of the streets of Cork – to be added later, no doubt.

'They followed him everywhere,' Fran said. 'After

he'd been cleared on the theft charge. And then, Hugo did ask for it in a way. He must have known the dangers of what he was setting in motion.'

'Fran! For God's sake!' Gareth exploded at last. 'Will you leave the subject alone?'

'No, I will not,' Fran said. 'These things have to be looked at from both sides. I'm not saying the Rooneys had any *right* to throw stones . . . '

'Damn you, Fran! Damn you!' Gareth leapt off the end of the bed. In his lunge at Fran, he caught hold of her hair. Moura and I stared at each other over her head – Fran was still kneeling by the video machine – then in embarrassment we looked away.

'You just mind your own business!' Gareth's voice came out in a choking scream, a noise that must have surprised him as much as it did us, because his eyes were round with alarm under eyebrows strained frantically up. 'He's my father and you don't say these things about him, do you hear? *Do you hear?*'

At first Fran looked rather amused, like a wealthy tourist in a foreign land who has been treated to an unexpected show of local manners. Then the grip on the hair grew more violent and a kick followed, aimed at Fran's behind as she half knelt on the floor.

'Gareth!' Moura said. 'Gareth, please!'

'Now get out of my house!' Gareth yelled at Fran. 'And don't come back!' But it was Gareth who ran out of the room after saying those words – and we heard him pound down the pebble corridor like a herd of cattle and slam and lock the door of his room.

'Well,' Fran said. Her face was an unusual colour, a whitish green with very bright spots under the cheekbones. With the black hair swinging she looked like a Dutch doll a child has just thrown against the wall. She turned to Moura, in an effort to recover dignity. 'I'm sorry, Moura,' she said.

I don't know if Fran saw the tiny shadow of a smile. Moura's smile was like the wrinkle on the sand at low tide when an invisible worm pushes up from underneath and is flattened out by a ripple of water. I saw it out of the corner of my eye. Then Moura's was a face of concern, of the double weight of a bereavement and a family row.

'I think we should all go to bed,' she said. 'We'll feel better in the morning.'

And she went out. Her head was high and the perfect neck was unbending. Her steps in the passage were quiet. We could just hear her go up the stairs to her room. So she hadn't gone to Gareth – Moura was too clever to play the mother now.

Fran sat back on her heels and gave a shaky smile. 'I've never seen Gareth like that,' she said. 'I didn't know he – he minded like that.' I watched Fran go from white-green back to normal colour again – and then to a healthy, greedy look, as if Gareth's outburst had proved an added bonus to the trip over here, a twinge of excitement in a relationship that was no longer exciting. She looked up at me from the floor, one arm resting on the video with a light familiarity – like women hold lightly on to their children in another's house.

'You don't think Gareth would – actually do anything, Minnie, do you?'

'Do anything?' I saw the new story forming, more dramatic by far than a simple mystery concerning Hugo's lack of judgment in old age. More enthralling even than the possible involvement of the younger Rooney brother in activities which Sally would deplore and Fran would praise. The actual revenge killing – by the son – of the dishonoured family . . . Fran's eyes were large and wondering.

'You told me what happened in the shop,' Fran said.

'Des Rooney punching him and all that. Moura was responsible for dropping the shirt, I take it?'

'I don't know,' I said stiffly.

'But maybe Gareth's . . . at the end of – I mean he does seem angry,' Fran said.

I rose from my chair. My own room all of a sudden seemed miles away down the corridor. I saw the tapestry, with the first, faint rustle of movement in the woods coming out to me in the silence. A horse's hoof rose and fell. A heap of faded, orange leaves shifted in the near trees.

'I'm going to bed,' I said.

'Oh Minnie, we've hardly talked.' Fran got up too and patted the bed. She went and sat on the end of it, where Gareth had been. 'You haven't asked about Philip's new wife. Aren't you interested? You used to be lovers, after all.'

I felt myself smiling. 'There's been too much else on my mind, I suppose. Tell me about her, Fran. Is she like you?'

Fran considered. 'Well, you could say so, I suppose. She's a publisher – an Editor-in-Chief, to be exact.' Fran mentioned a famous American publishing company. 'Maybe it helped, when she started, that her father owned it. But she rose on her own merits. Entirely,' Fran said.

'Just like you, Fran,' I said. 'I hope the marriage will get Philip nearer where he wants to be.'

'And where's that?' Fran looked slightly surprised.

'Back here, of course. This place is everything to him.'

'Really?' Fran now became thoughtful. 'He must be a dark horse. He's hardly mentioned here. He seems to – kind of – belong all over the place – he travels so much, I suppose.'

Why would he tell you? I felt like saying. But I don't

want to insult Fran. What's the point, after all: these things, as Moura used to say, look after themselves. 'Oh, Philip was forced to leave here by Hugo,' I said all the same. 'Hugo wanted him to repeat his own brilliant youth in America – his career – everything. Philip always wanted to stay here, but Hugo would have disapproved. Now he's – not here – Hugo I mean . . .'

'You think Philip'll come and live here?' Fran laughed. 'I don't see Araminta taking life in a hole like this. She has ambitious plans for the future. When Philip isn't doing his pieces on world politics they'll be building up a new publishing house together. An imprint she can really feel is her own, not her father's, you know.'

Fran sounded gushing I thought, like a Vassar girl in a movie. I sat by her on the end of the bed – out of a memory of our old friendship – to show I didn't mind how she went on. Although we were older we could still play girls-together if we felt in the mood.

'I'm sure he'll come,' I said. 'And come to stay.'

'To stay?' Fran swivelled sideways on the bed to look at me. I could see fine lines round her eyes – lines you can't see unless you come up very close.

'Philip's on his honeymoon,' Fran said. She frowned. 'He could be back by now, I suppose. But if he was back he'd have come over.' She looked at me now with frank curiosity. I felt that dangerous warmth – when the professional interviewer turns all her interest on you. But I resisted the temptation.

'Why are you so sure of Philip coming?' Fran asked.

I smiled. 'He can come and be with me at last,' I said. 'Now Hugo's dead. It was Hugo, you know, who wouldn't let Philip marry me.' I felt warmer still – but Fran's eyes were so interested: she was deeply involved with all I said. 'Of course, Hugo was a fascinating man,' I said. 'But ruthless. He had a future planned out for Philip – it didn't include a girl like me – and I dare say he must've minded that Philip didn't marry earlier. He probably knew Philip didn't want to. Now – well, I'm sure Philip can get his book published by the new wife in America . . . ' I broke off, heard myself laugh. 'But he'll be living here. With me. Hugo's not here to stop it any more.'

Fran got up and went to the window. She tugged at the curtain. 'Did you hear anything just then, Minnie?'

'Hear anything?' I was disagreeably jolted from what had seemed a cosy conversation. But then, Fran, you can pull any trick in the book.

'Footsteps outside on the gravel,' Fran said. 'I could have sworn I heard footsteps.'

We both listened. There was complete silence. I felt my warmth drain away. I got up – rather unsteady – my legs had bent under me on the bed. 'Well Fran . . .' I began.

Fran was still frowning as she came to the door of her room and she looked out after me as I went down the corridor. She followed, keeping her voice low. 'I can't understand it, Minnie,' she said.

'What?' I let Fran catch me up. She stood with me now in my doorway. The lamp was on and the tapestry glowed dimly at the far end of the room. She lowered her voice although it wasn't necessary – Lily sleeps on the other side of the house and Moura up behind fortress walls.

'Philip always told me it was Moura who wouldn't let him marry you,' Fran said. 'He told me Moura threatened to cut him out of Cliff Hold if he married you. She told him you were unstable, or something. But I said to Philip that that wasn't fair. It just so happened that I'd known you when we were at film school together. You'd had an unbalanced childhood – you'd been moved around a lot – but I said you were just fine.'

Friday, 3.30 p.m.

It's been an uneven kind of a day today. A speckled sky, which looks as if it's had a bowl of milk thrown over it – and sudden bursts of rain making puddles so wide the orange cats stand and stare at each other over the muddy water. It started raining last night; by now, with most of the rain sunk into the grass, you can hardly see the tyre marks where the car swerved before crashing into the side of the house. There's a channel of bright mud up by the gates, it's true – it looks as if some prehistoric animal had lashed its tail on its walk over the south of the country. The car itself looks absurd, a crumpled-up pile of blue metal by the side of the window of Gareth's room. The other car, an identical Ford Escort that Fran hired at the airport, is still parked neatly up by the gates. If you look straight ahead and you don't see Gareth's car in its state of monstrous wreckage, you can pretend things are as they always were – when there was just one car, of course, before Fran came.

I still don't know what to say. Was it the rain that came down in a sound of racing engines in my sleep – or did I wake and go to the window, standing in the dark room by the tapestry where the noble family ride to hounds in a wood obscured by night? Did I after all hear footsteps outside last night – when I thought it was just Fran trying to distract me? I did look out – after Fran had gone safely to bed – was it a shadow I saw or was it Moura, flying up the path in a white nightdress and a black shiny mac? And didn't the faint light from the passage indoors catch the shiny mac, which she wears to lop at plants in her tropical garden;

154

and wasn't her face turned towards the gates? If I know I lifted my window, quietly, quietly, and slid on to the sopping grass; if I'm sure it was Moura who prowled round the cars, trying to decide which car to pick, which was the right one for her plan; then shouldn't I have said so already to Gareth? Instead I've stayed in my room all day, except for when Lily called me an hour ago to say Moura wanted some help with the preparations for the Games. Shouldn't I have said that I ran on the wet grass while Moura turned on blinding headlights in the car (by mistake, obviously), and I danced in the arc of light for a few seconds like a moth? But maybe I was lying asleep after all and the rain drummed on the windows and I never saw Moura at all. Who crashed the car then? Was it really as she made out?

Gareth was so appalled by the deliberate vandalizing of the car that he spent most of the morning walking round and round the wreck, as if he owned the car or had been attached to it in some way. Fran kept to herself: when she did emerge from her room it was with a serious air – she was always clutching a notebook or a file – and I think for the first time Gareth respected her attitude to events. Anything was better than Lily's low, pious prayers or Moura's portentous looks – and hints that she had looked out of her window and 'seen someone up by the gate'. It may have been, too, that Gareth wanted to believe in Fran's theory – viz., that the destruction of the car was a political act of terrorism, leading on from Fran's 'discovery' of the possible involvement of the younger Rooney in acts of violence in the North – that Fran's visit to the newspaper office in Cork and her questioning of reporters and the public (in bars, in parks, even as close to home as Dunane) had brought a swift warning. He didn't want to think that this 'mindless violence' as he called it again and again in the long, shocked morning, could possibly be the result of Hugo's investigations into petty crime and domestic strife.

Even so, the swollen, angry face of Des Rooney in Ryan's must have come back to him. I could see, each time I went to my window and stood by the tapestry and looked out, that poor Gareth was trying to make up his mind as to what he should do. He could hardly leave now – abandon his mother to danger – but this was what he wanted to do, I know. I saw how cleverly Moura had anchored him here, by insisting he take his old nurse to the Games. Then I heard him asking Fran urgently whether they shouldn't get back before things got any worse here. He pretended he suggested this for the safety of Fran: surely they should avoid further provocation – and wasn't she being provocative, by poking her cameras into a business that was better left alone? Fran laughed. I stood like a ghost by my window, still slightly open from my climb out on to the grass the night before. (Or had I been sleepwalking? Did I dream I walked on the smooth grass which minutes later would be seared by the wheels of the car?) As Fran laughed I shivered. I could tell she was mocking Gareth's cowardice – cornering him further into that impassive, neutral world to which he seemed now completely to belong.

'Don't let them get away with it,' Fran said.

'What on earth d'you mean?' I heard a terrified realization in Gareth's voice: that his mother and his wife, just as much as a mother and wife in a border castle in mediaeval times, were determined that Gareth should 'act as a man'. They couldn't really mean he was to go out and kill, of course – but he was supposed to do *something*. Fran, the newest of New Women, had come alive at Gareth's first outburst of

156

violent rage last night. And it was true that as I stood there, under the scene of ritualized violence, of torn beasts and spears and the stain of red woven blood on the tapestry in my room, I too felt a twinge of contempt for Gareth. Yet what did I expect him to do? And isn't it still my duty to go to him and say it was Moura who crashed his car last night? She'll do anything for her vengeance now.

'I mean, we have to get the Guards and find out who did that to the car,' came Fran's practical voice. 'And then you take the Rooneys to court.'

Gareth was silent. I could almost hear him thinking: a future either of quick violence or of long-drawn-out lawsuits lies ahead. And I can't bear either. But he didn't say anything at all.

'Anyway, we must be here tomorrow,' Fran said. 'It's the Games. We can take Lily over in my car. You know how long Moura's kept her here without seeing her brother, Gareth? It's really disgraceful.'

Good-deeds, altruistic Fran as well as brilliant, investigative, successful Fran. I swallowed hard and turned back from the window to my bed. But then I found myself smiling: Gareth is pinned down doubly now. Both his mother and his wife will make sure he stays at Cliff Hold – and takes Lily to the Games.

Friday, 6.30 p.m.
Something will go badly wrong at the Games tomorrow. I can feel it – I'm sure Lily can feel it, because she had a distant, worried look on her face when I went into the kitchen an hour ago – and on the day before the Games she's usually laughing, saying she's sure the Murphy child will be tripping everyone up in the three-legged race – or Mrs Ryan is too fat to go in for the fancy-dress parade – things like that. Instead, she

looked at me as if I was just another possible problem, putting her head on one side as mute as Old Tom in her refusal to answer an unspoken question.

'Lily,' I said. 'Is it – is it going to be a fine day tomorrow?'

'I don't order the weather now, do I, Minnie?' she said.

'No, but you can usually tell . . .'

'I can tell one thing.' Lily moved to the sink and picked up a long scrubbing-brush that was eaten away in the middle. 'The birds will learn a lesson or two and high time.'

'The birds?' I had a vague memory of Moura saying all the currants and strawberries were under attack from birds this year. 'At Blackstone?' I said. 'What kind of lesson?'

'You'll see,' Lily said. 'If Mr Henry and Miss Ottoline weren't half asleep most of the time there'd be something done about it already. And Mrs Pierce had a job with the gardeners, to get them to work before every berry was off the trees.'

I saw Moura on her horse, on the way back from our ride to Ardo, bending down at the gatehouse and talking to the old men who had worked all their lives on the land at Blackstone. Something as vague as a shadow passed in front of my eyes. A fear pain followed – in a white blur – to the head.

'Surely they won't go for the birds on the one day it's the Games?' I said. 'I mean, wouldn't it be dangerous?'

Lily finished scrubbing the wooden inside of the sink. The mangy brush went back with a thud in the dish. I saw how small Lily was when she spoke with her back to me like that: her shoulders were narrow, her back short and thin under the white overalls. I felt another pain – of loss, of a childhood when Lily had

158

been tall and I had swung on what seemed to me then to be powerful arms.

'Dangerous for the birds,' Lily said. The wooden sink gave off its sudsy, wet smell. Lily found an encrusted pie-dish next, to plunge in boiling water. She wouldn't turn to face me – I know Lily. So I went back to my room, and lay on my bed, and stared.

Of course I must go and tell Gareth. I come over to Cliff Hold after ten years, I find the family dispersed, Hugo murdered, Moura on the edge of madness, and I enter it all without a thought for the consequences. It's as if I was determined to walk into the tapestry that hangs opposite me as I write – where already, through the trees, I see the sloping hill down to Blackstone, the formal stitching of the vegetables in the garden, the pale billow of the marquee where they serve lemonade and food. As I go I see the change of movements of the people on the wall – the hunters and the hunted and the wayfarers who get caught up by accident in the final stages of the kill. I leave Gareth to think all night that his enemies came to the house and crashed his car – something will go badly wrong at the Games tomorrow – I'm sure of that. But something stops me from going along the passage to Gareth. Since the episode of the car, he's become pale, withdrawn; he lies coughing on his bed and doesn't get up; and his coughs are like strangled cries of protest and fear.

PART THREE

Birds. As I look from the kitchen window I see the birds – white and wide-winged, they look too big to be gulls – that have swooped over Cliff Hold in the last two days, screeching, marking out the end of summer. The Guards have gone down the passage. I hear the crunch of their boots on the pebbles. Moura, still with her bright, mystified look, has stepped out to the staircase garden. A high wind – which blew away the clouds and let through a too-gold sun, rattles the palm fronds and turns Lily's hair to a blur of white. Pains like pins and needles run in the tips of my fingers. Moura just said to me, 'You shouldn't have been mixed up in this, Minnie. Why not go home to your mother now?' But the North Kensington street with its market and wine bar and the fusty apartment with the smell of exercise books is too far away for me to get back to now. Besides, Moura, I want to stay with you.

It was the birds that made me lose Gareth. He wasn't in his room when I went to look for him, and by the time I'd gone out of the gates to look for him in the lane, the birds had changed to black birds – crows, rooks, sitting in a row – on a telegraph wire just above the fuchsia which bled under them so the whole lane cawed with menace. I didn't want to go up to the left, where the lane gets narrow. I saw the dust and I saw Gareth walking in a haze of dust, scissored by the

163

Rooneys. In the hedges the onlookers peered: Hugo's people, and history. The Rooneys, in suits as black as crows and with padded shoulders, came in on either side of Gareth. If the younger brother stood for Hugo's political beliefs – for freedom, anarchy, violence justified by the urgency of rebellion – the elder one closed in on Hugo's son with the blows of greed, lust, corruption. I saw Gareth fall – the dust-mirage disappeared – but by then I was down the garden, trembling – looking for Moura to calm me out of one of my states, as she's always done.

Moura was sorting jumble in the garden shed. The stall at the Games was every year piled high with old junk from Cliff Hold. I recognized, dimly, a stuffed elephant with most of the stuffing gone and a cane saddle in the shape of a seat – we must have gone on donkey-rides on the sand strapped in it, I suppose.

'Moura,' I said, 'I didn't tell you before. Philip got married in New York.'

Moura pulled glass beads off a moth-eaten piece of string and they fell neatly through her fingers into a jar.

'That's why he's not here. He never sent the cable. Fran sent it.'

Moura looked up at me. Her expression was charming, as if she had just been paid a compliment on her garden. 'Thank you, Minnie,' she said. 'I didn't for one minute think Philip had sent the cable.'

The stopper for the jar was too small. Moura made a wad of tissue paper to fill out the space. I wondered who would want a jar of beads. Babies would eat them. A bright blue bead, blue as a worry bead or the eye of an icon, stared out at me from the jar.

'Don't you want to know who he married?' I said.

Moura made the sideways tilt of her head that gives her the look of a madonna, in white plaster and with

164

blue robes: a madonna you see in Victorian nurseries, high on the wall.

'Philip rang this afternoon,' she said. 'He's arriving tomorrow. I told him to go straight to Blackstone.' She smiled. 'It'll be ages since he's been at the Games.'

'Didn't he say he was married?' I said before I could take this in. 'She's a friend of Fran's.'

The jar of beads tipped over. We pushed them back as best we could.

Moura didn't reply. I helped her with the rest of the junk. It had to be loaded into bin-liners and carried up to her old car by the gates. We didn't look down at the house, at Gareth's bright, crumpled car against the wall. I didn't ask if the act of vandalism had been reported yet and Moura didn't ask me where Gareth was. The jar of beads spilled out again into the boot, I remember. The tissue paper plug hadn't been strong enough. Moura tut-tutted with irritation at the loose, rolling beads.

The Guards come back into the kitchen. Lily is stooped at the sink, scrubbing quietly and so rhythmically it's easy to think she's not there at all. And it's true, the Guards are distracted first by Moura's arrangement of red flowers, of dahlias and the early, burnt-coloured chrysanthemums, which have a stronger presence than Lily and are arranged in the middle of the room on a plinth Moura likes to use for formal occasions. But I can't think what the formal occasion can be going to be.

One of the Guards – the younger one with a gentle face – evidently knows Lily. He says, 'Lily, can we be having a word with you please?' And she turns at the sink like a piece of clockwork, as if she'd just been waiting to hear them say her name.

The birds followed us all the way to Blackstone on the morning of the Games. It was Saturday, yesterday, when Moura took me in her car – Gareth and Fran had already left in Fran's car, she said, because Fran didn't want to miss the filming of the opening speech. We were missing it on purpose, I knew, because it had been Hugo's amusement, once, to give it – and now it would be Cousin Henry making a hash of it – very amusing for Fran's New York audience, no doubt. We left the hall, with Moura's trampled flower basket still pointedly in the corner – and one lumber-jack anorak still on the peg. How like Fran, I thought, to walk unencumbered at the Games – tall, in her jeans and shirt, while Gareth walks behind her and coughs, well-covered.

Moura gave me an affectionate shove as I stood by the front door, looking out, day-dreaming, gazing up at the clipped peacocks that have grown so tall and shaggy since I was last here. 'Come on, Minnie, don't dawdle, we'll be late for the Games!' I'd heard her say that every year when I was a child. And I stepped back and nearly upset the coats on the stand. 'What a shame Fran left her camera,' I said, when I felt the hard edge of her anorak – and I thought: it'll be tactless to tell Moura, but I'll take it along and give it to Fran. And Moura called, as I struggled up the drive after her: 'Come *on*, Minnie, we'll be late!'

We drove slowly, under a sky thick with birds. Even Moura frowned, at the sheer numbers of crows and rooks that came down from their holding patterns and settled on fences and trees, and on the new stubble in the fields.

'It's the harvest,' she said. 'Luckily, at Blackstone, we've got the guns.'

And I smiled and nodded agreement at Moura's profile. But something in me knew she was thinking of guns brought to the door by a child. Guns from the Gun Room left purposely unlocked for Old Tom and the child to go in.

'Bird-guns,' Moura said. 'Scarecrows are not the answer in the garden, as I've told them again and again.'

Lily walks out of the kitchen with a Guard on either side. How tiny they make her look. They're showing her into Hugo's study; it's the desk and chair in there, I suppose, that makes them want to do their questioning in that room, but there's an irony, too, about an investigation of the innocent taking place in the room where Hugo wrote his coolly impassioned novels about freedom and innocence and guilt.

I can't hear Lily's voice, but it sounds as if she's burst into tears.

By the time Moura and I got to Blackstone the Games were in full swing. A band played on the sunken lawn under the yews. The three-legged race was half-way round its course. There seemed to be more people than usual – or am I just less able to bear crowds than when I was young? I couldn't see Lily, who must have been taken there by Gareth and Fran. I couldn't see Gareth or Fran either. Cousin Henry had spotted us, though, and came unsteadily up. 'Made a bit of a mess of my speech,' he told Moura. 'It turned out to be a sermon a visiting clergyman had left in the Yellow Bedroom in 1911!'

Moura didn't laugh. I could see she was scanning the sports. Her eye went impatiently over the tables with jumble and the arrays of potted plants and cuttings, and the booth where a fat woman was selling candy floss. She stared at the entrance to the kitchen garden, hidden by the west wing of the house.

'Is everything going well?' she asked Cousin Henry in a formal voice.

I suppose I couldn't bear it. Somewhere, in that crowd of people who didn't matter – in that mass of floral hats and red faces, Philip must be standing. By a stall – looking out for his mother. Laughing, pretending to join in a tombola. Finding the old junk from the nursery at Blackstone – remembering me.

But it was Gareth I saw. I picked him out because I recognized the lumber-jack anorak and wondered why he had the hood up. Did he expect it to rain? He was walking up by the west wing of Blackstone and making for the entrance to the kitchen garden. I followed him.

In the frame of its crumbling, brick walls the garden stood as still and faded as the tapestry on the wall of my room at Cliff Hold. Beyond the furthest wall, where Old Tom's cottage was half embedded in a width of brick as fat as a kiln, I could see trees moving their branches in the wind. But there was no wind in the garden of decayed vegetables and hedges half seas over, their underbelly of twigs poking up at the sky. There was an old handkerchief tied to one of the raspberry canes – as if someone had thought of making a scarecrow and then given up. I thought of the bird-guns. I saw the tapestry in my room go still and quiet, like the day the violence moved into the house. I heard the wind – and steps in my room in the early morning when it was still so dark that Moura could come and take the canvas bag I had hidden away from her, on the night the child came to the door with fish. She could walk out of the room with the bag a pale shadow beside her – while the wind got up and doors slammed and windows rattled – and I saw, I'm beginning to see, Moura, a row of coats in the hall – and your hand, hardly visible because it's still so dark –

and the gun in your hand as it slides into the pocket of Gareth's anorak.

Gareth walked into the kitchen garden and stood still. It was absolutely quiet, with the only sound the bee-drone that carries you back to the past. Maybe Gareth thought of his childhood too as he stood there. Then the first bird-gun went off. I saw Gareth whip round. Another gun detonated. Gareth fell to his knees on the weedy path as if he'd been hurt. The hood of the anorak hid his face from me. I stayed, quiet as a mouse, behind the box hedge and out of sight of the gate.

Oh, I should have known! It was like watching a play where half the lines and the action have been learned by heart and the rest is made up as the players go along. I knew only not to move – to keep still in my corner, back pressed up against the rusty wire of a now-dead pear-tree. I was at right angles to Old Tom's cottage. Out he came – on time, on a cue I couldn't see – to the stage Moura had built for him. The child and the dog came out after Old Tom. Then the child ran to the gate and into the garden, where the Games were getting every minute noisier – a voice on a loudspeaker announced the egg-and-spoon race, a woman screamed and there was laughter.

Gareth got up off his knees and walked towards Old Tom. With the hood of the anorak up, he looked from behind like a puzzled, overgrown boy. And when Old Tom held up a cabbage leaf to his mouth, Gareth stopped and stood still – as if he was just beginning to realize he had walked into a play – only, in his case, as his hesitant stance showed only too clearly, he hadn't had any idea of what the part was to be.

The band struck up suddenly. I don't know why – but the music sounded brutal, over-loud. Under its blare, the kitchen garden seemed to grow fainter, to inch back in time – to a time when the sound of

169

Oklahoma! could never have penetrated the crumbling walls and neat box hedges, low and ammonia-smelling. I saw dimly, as the child came in through the gates again. The Rooneys were in a haze of sound and heat as they followed the child (what had Moura rehearsed the child to lure them in with?). They went half-way up the kitchen garden – and I saw Old Tom as he stood with the cabbage leaf over his face by his cottage door. They turned to the side and saw Gareth. The dog barked, and another volley of bird-guns went off. They ran. To the gap in the brick wall. They jumped – the smaller one let out a curse of pain – and they were through. They were on the hill that leads up to the hills at Ardo. Gareth swung away from Old Tom and raced after them.

The Guards are sitting at the kitchen table as if they had all the time in the world. The younger one admires the orange flowers. Yes, says Moura, stiff and remote again. They are nice aren't they? And could you tell me please what you've been talking to my maid about?

'Lily was telling us,' the older Guard said, 'that Mr Gareth was here in the house all day. She said she was here herself and she never went to the Games. Is that right, Mrs Pierce?'

'Yes, that's right,' Moura said. 'I had to go, you see. Well, obviously. Lily had to be here to let the doctor in. A shame . . . but . . . ' Moura's voice tails off; she sounds bored with the subject '. . . these things happen,' she ends vaguely.

'And did the doctor come?' the Guard asks – and I listen to Gareth's cough at the end of the passage – and I see: Moura didn't let him go to the Games. So – who –

'Oh yes, sure the doctor came,' Lily says. 'And you've only to ring him for him to say so.'

A silence. What have they been asking Lily in Hugo's room? They look stunned, like police in a comedy: Moura has outwitted us all.

Then, a car on the gravel outside. It's a relief to hear Sally's voice, booming closer as she lets herself in the front door. But Moura looks up. Absurdly, she looks irritated, as if a gatecrasher had arrived at one of her more successful parties.

'What is Sally doing here?' she says.

Moura – I should have seen the moment you changed your mind. It was in the garden shed, wasn't it? When I told you Philip had married a friend of Fran's – and you couldn't take any of it any longer. Fran, her cameras, your two stolen sons, a future without Hugo and without respect. It was while you were piling the old toys, the junk from the nursery at Cliff Hold, that you thought of using her. If there was to be danger – and you'd made sure there had to be – then why shouldn't Fran be the one to be exposed to it? You held up a broken lorry, a cloth elephant both the boys had loved. Why should Gareth be at risk, carrying out the revenge you had promised to yourself and your honour? And I saw you look down at the glass jar of beads, and almost as if on purpose, knock it to the side so it fell and the beads rolled out. I saw you look at the blue bead – it rolled away from us in the boot of the car, too – as blue and round and elusive as your mother's eye.

By the time I'd run through the gap in the brick wall and up the hill to the woods at Ardo, a quiet had settled which smelt of waiting and fear. I was in the tapestry. I had no place there. I stood in the leaves – on the outskirts of the wood – and stared down at my feet. They were half buried in leaves so coppery they looked as if they'd been sprayed with paint. I wanted to go.

171

But if there was a sudden movement – I knew it like an animal – there'd be violence.

The Rooneys were the first to move. They couldn't stand the suspense – perhaps – or they too wanted to run from ground swept free of leaves under the trees where Hugo had fallen and died. They came out separately, about fifty yards apart. Right on the far side of the wood – where it slopes down away from Blackstone, to the path we rode over on our way from Cliff Hold. They were so far from me that I could tell only that Des Rooney was shot first – because he was the bigger and taller, and he fell suddenly like a fat cardboard cat at a fun fair. The smaller one put up his arms. But another shot rang out, and he fell too.

Moura is looking with her sad, pious, beautiful face at the Guards. I see, this morning, our casual departure for the Games, the one anorak on the peg in the hall – Gareth's of course: he was told to stay in bed and nurse his cough. By you, Moura. And it was you who slipped into my room in the early morning and found the canvas bag I thought I'd hidden from you in the cupboard under the tapestry. You took the bag – and you took out the gun – but you made a terrible mistake. I half upset the coats as we were about to leave for the Games – do you remember, Moura, I was always clumsy like that as a child – but then it got worse – and you didn't see that Fran had taken the wrong coat after all. She was in Gareth's coat – Gareth's innocent coat, with nothing hard in the pocket, put there earlier by you. But you don't know that – poor Moura, do you?

Moura turns her sad smile on the Guards. 'I wonder if anyone has seen Fran,' she says. '*Mrs* Gareth Pierce. She was at the Games – most certainly.'

There's something so filmic about the woods at Ardo. That's what I thought as I climbed up into the dead leaves and stood under a dappled tree only a couple of hundred yards from Fran. Something in the red and the gold – and the soft swell of green hill that leads down to the kitchen garden at Blackstone. It all looks unreal, and bright – and as if you could shoot it again and again and it would always stay the same, whatever the season. I suppose it must be because of the beech leaves, which never change their colour – even if they've been lying under the trees dead, all the year through.

Moura must have got Old Tom and the gardeners to fix up the bird-guns in the woods. I was frightened at first, by the bang – but then I can film in any conditions. It's easy, really – as long as you learn to concentrate.

No problem here, either. The trees looked as beautiful in the lens as I thought they would. But everything was bigger, like a telescope. I was frightened, too, the second I saw how big the men were – so big they must have been running towards me. If it hadn't been for that bang of the bird-gun, Moura, I'd never have found the courage to press on the trigger and kill. And you know – the maddening thing – my long hair kept swinging over the viewfinder and nearly blocked my sights altogether. My long, black hair. But then I found myself bursting out in laughter. It wasn't my hair at all – it was just my eyes blurring over, making fine hairs like grey cracks in the glass of the lens. It was over so quickly. First the big one fell. Then the smaller one, near him. It was lucky in the end, Moura, that I was the one who acted for you. Did you really think I would allow Fran to take the coat with the gun? Of course she can use her camera any time she wants – but she looked too surprised in the woods at Ardo, to contemplate getting anything on film. She'd followed her 'investigative' nose; run after the Rooneys up to the wood – and all the while I thought she was Gareth! – then, she was caught unawares! Anyway, would

Fran shoot with a gun? She hasn't the nerve – even in self-defence. But for that second I knew what it was to have her power, to hold the world in a frame and freeze it dead.

Now I sit with Moura. All the fuss and disturbance has died down – the Guards have gone, and Sally – Sally who seemed almost pleased at the news she brought. Maybe she felt Moura would be hers now, more fully – fall in with her plans, travel the world, rinse her hair blue. But Moura will never leave here now.

It was my fault, of course. When Sally came, with her heavy feet on the pebble passage and her flushed face round the door, I felt I knew what she had to tell – and the Guards looked to her, I thought, almost in gratitude. I went instinctively to stand by Moura's chair. I saw Lily's face patchy from weeping and I knew. It wasn't that the Guards had interrogated her fiercely in Hugo's room – they'd asked her nothing at all. But they'd told her the truth.

Gareth keeps coughing in his room at the end of the passage. We must buy him a linctus, when Moura feels well enough to go down to Dunane. Does he know his brother's dead? No – he can't know yet – leave him, Moura said.

Sally told the news with her stout arms held out at her side and her head erect. 'It wasn't the two Rooneys who were shot, Moura,' she said. 'It was Des Rooney all right. His brother had already run away. But – the other – Moura, Philip is dead.'

You could say that Philip was looking for his father first – for the spot anyway, where Hugo fell. Then he would go back down to Blackstone – to the Games, the music, the long meadows where his mother had lived as a child. He would find his mother and they would kiss – as Lily used to say, Philip was the apple of his mother's eye. But Philip had loved Hugo. He would go first to the tall orange trees . . . walking up the hill as the band in the garden at Blackstone played *Oklahoma* . . . he would go to the far side of the wood, the side nearest the way down to Cliff Hold. He'd see the bald mounds of earth, where the leaves had been raked away after Hugo's fall. And he'd step out, unknowing, at the same time as Des Rooney, into a patch of sunlight in the floor of the wood. Des Rooney must have made the start of a run – but the bird-gun went off – and then another shot – and he fell, dead. Philip put his arms up. But he was shot down too.

Sunday, September 8th

Addio. Philip wouldn't have remembered anyway. I promised Moura when the Guards and Sally left that I wouldn't daydream any more – it's my worst fault. And I told her how much I admired her plan, and the care she'd taken to execute it properly. I said I'd never tell the Guards.

Oh, poor Moura! Your eldest son, Philip, the apple of your eye. It was my fault. I'll never leave you now.

You see, Moura, I know Philip went to the woods at Ardo to find me. He didn't want to remember Hugo – Hugo never thought of me with real affection. Philip wasn't looking for the place where Hugo fell. He was looking for the mound of leaves where we lay together – that day I promised to stay near the house at Blackstone – while you took sketches of the fruit in the kitchen garden. Do you remember, Moura? Philip wasn't looking for you, either, at the Games or in the old house at Blackstone. You stopped him from marrying me. He didn't want to find you at all. He was looking for me. It was my fault, Moura: he flew into your ambush and he fell.

175

Lily came in a minute ago, and said did we want some tea? The episode of the china pot is all forgotten; we'll use the old brown one on the top shelf of the dresser – the one Lily used when we were children. You said you didn't want any, Moura – but you must try to eat and drink. I remember, I felt like you after that last summer at Cliff Hold – when my mother drove me to the place outside London and guns went off in my head. Then I didn't feel like eating or drinking, either. But in the end it passed.

The Guards came in again. Moura looked up at them with that sad smile – but with hope in her eyes, too. 'Have you found Fran?' she says quietly, as if everything is going to be solved and soon we're going to be able to enjoy our tea in peace. 'Oh yes,' the older of the Guards says. 'She's out in the car and she's all right, Mrs Pierce, I'm happy to say.'

'All right?' Moura looks down now, uncertain.

'It's you we'd like to come with us,' the younger one says to me.

'Minnie?' Moura stares, as if she's forgotten again that I am there.

I must get up. I must go. But I don't want to leave Cliff Hold. For one thing, Moura, you're alone here now. It was cruel of you, Fran, to tell the Guards to come for me.

'Go home to your mother,' Moura shouts suddenly. I've never heard her use that voice before. 'Your mother always said you were wrong for Philip. She said you hung on here far too long!'

I turn and see Lily looking at me. Then Lily looks away. But, Moura, I don't want to go home, to the market and the wine bar and the fusty apartment with the smell of exercise books. You know my mother wasn't a real mother to me. I've got to stay here, Moura, and keep an eye on you!